THE FLOATING GAME

Emma Peel found Steed floating in a tank of water with his breathing apparatus leading into his rubber suit like an umbilical cord.

She kicked Curt Krystal as he came up the stairs towards her, and then she felt her way through the folds of flesh in his neck to stop the blood to his head. He fainted without more than a grunt. But now Emma was angry. Steed had mufflers over his eyes and ears, things like boxing gloves on his hands to kill the sense of touch, and she knew what this treatment did to the mind.

She turned to face the three Chinese girls, feeling very ruthless. . . .

"The Floating Game"

JOHN GARFORTH

A novel based on the ABC-TV
series THE AVENGERS

A BERKLEY MEDALLION BOOK
Published by
BERKLEY PUBLISHING CORPORATION

BERKLEY MEDALLION EDITION, APRIL, 1967

BERKLEY MEDALLION BOOKS are published by Berkley Publishing Corporation 15 East 26th Street, New York, N.Y. 10010

BERKLEY MEDALLION BOOKS ® TM 757,375

Printed in the United States of America

1

He wanted to look decent when they found him. No point in being found dead in underpants. He hoped he wouldn't be sick either. . . . Sir Arthur selected a floppy bow tie with restrained flecks of mauve across it, and then spent a tedious four minutes tying it. He smiled wryly—yes, wryly, that was the word, as he reflected that he wouldn't need to struggle with ties again.

Astonishing how calm you are, once you've really decided! All those fears and confusions are at last gone. He was rather pleased with himself for his consideration towards the police. "I do hope I shan't be sick," he said aloud. It was like standing outside yourself and watching that poor, miserable, slightly disgusting fool solve his problems, as if it were of purely academic interest.

Sir Arthur went through into the lounge. It wouldn't hurt, of course, he had made sure of that. The bottle of whisky was already half empty, and he poured himself another glass. He stood by the uncurtained window and looked across Westminster to the House of Commons. He could just see the top of Big Ben between office blocks, and the red light indicated that the House was still sitting. Ah well, he would not be perorating in there again either. Sir Arthur Smeck-Hudson, M.P. Deceased.

It was snowing as well, but that didn't matter. Nothing mattered now, so long as it didn't hurt. The harsh light reflected from the snow, the bleak night scene, was curiously appropriate to his mood. Sir Arthur turned indifferently back into his lounge. He ought to be thinking of the suicide note, before he was too fuddled to compose it correctly.

My life has become intolerable. But who was he writing this for? He had no wife to care whether he lived or died, no woman who loved him. No friends worthy of the name. Tamara? Not now. He hadn't seen his relatives in years. The only people who would care would be those he owed money to, and the M.I.5. Dear Policeman. It is better this way. I can't bear the idea of dragging my name and profession down into the gutter. . . .

Politics had killed his feeling for language. How could he express what his life had become? Sir Arthur knocked back another glass of whisky. He felt as if he had been running in blind panic, running day after day, evading disaster this time and this time, but always knowing that either tomorrow or next week it would all be over. Getting into debt, borrowing, gambling, and losing, stealing, and then. . . . He tore up the letter. For more than a year now every time the doorbell rang he had half-expected it to be the end.

There are no words to express what you feel when your life has been thrown away. And a man of fifty seven doesn't cry. Well, not any more. He began counting the tablets in the bottle, lining them up in ranks like white soldiers in a surgery. There seemed to be forty-three although he couldn't be sure. He was beginning to feel distinctly intoxicated. Sloshed. Bloody glad to be shot of it all. As long as it didn't—. All right, I'm a coward.

I'm committing suicide to avoid a public scandal and national disgrace. He had been a fool and this was the only decent way to end it. Like a Roman. Sir Arthur found tears welling up in his eyes again. And as he thought self-pityingly about those distinguished years before he met Tamara they trickled ridiculously down his cheeks. He had been rich, successful, dignified . . . and now he was shabby, squalid and embarrassing.

Sir Arthur put the first tablet in his mouth, rinsed the whisky about it for a moment and then swallowed. A second tablet, then a third. So this was it.

Supposing that death itself hurts? You know, that split second of time when you cross the threshold— when life is suddenly extinguished. It might be torn from you like a strip of flesh.

The fifteenth tablet wouldn't go down. And he was feeling sick. Sir Arthur walked unsteadily to the winged armchair and sat gazing into the fire. He'd taken enough to kill him twice over, but he wanted to be sure. He took another five, drowsily, and then carried on staring into the fire. His heart seemed to be beating like a drum and his brain was pulsating wildly.

He didn't hear the doorbell.

When the man in the black suit came into the room Sir Arthur could scarcely focus on his face. And the voice was another world away. But it didn't seem to be very important. The fellow was prowling about, looking at the tablets and taking the half-written letter from the wastepaper basket.

"I'm glad you're being sensible about all this," the voice called through a long, reverberating tunnel.

"Gimme the whisky."

"Certainly. Perhaps I'll join you." He poured the rest of the bottle into two glasses and then raised his own in a toast. "To that old fashioned British sense of decency, yes?" The fellow was laughing at him.

"Lea' m'alone."

"No, really, I'm very pleased with you. You're so sensible. I came here tonight to kill you, and you've saved me a lot of conscience pangs. I shall now sleep untroubled. Excellent whisky as well."

The slow deliberate chimes of Big Ben rolled out across the world and Sir Arthur counted foolishly up to eleven. They belonged to an England he understood, where Westminster represented traditional authority and Eton stood for eternal values and the Church welded together an empire, when an officer was a gentleman and *The Times* was the voice of the age. He should never have strayed into the nineteen sixties.

It was eleven o'clock and Sir Arthur was feeling

confused. His body was pitching about and yet he couldn't be sure what was hurting. Something was killing him. He muttered. He wanted to say that he was frightened. But he didn't mean to slobber like a baby. He had wanted to make it a dignified ending. The man in the black suit drained his glass and replaced it on the silver tray. His job was done, so he walked silently across the piled carpet, drew the heavy curtains and turned out the light at the door. The firelight reflected a dull red on the oak panelling of the walls. An elaborate portrait of a dancer stared down at him in the hall and the man shrugged his shoulders apologetically. Sir Arthur Smeck-Hudson had had to die. He let himself out quietly.

2

"Sir Arthur Smeck-Hudson, or—as his intimates called him affectionately, S.H., was a man whose life was dedicated to public service. He was a soldier and a statesman, fighting for those ideals he believed in whatever the personal cost, against communism in Spain, against fascism when the time came, and against socialism when the war was over. He will be remembered by his numerous friends and thousands of grateful constituents . . ."

Funeral orations are always boring, either unnecessary or untrue. John Steed leaned idly against the heavy church door and surveyed the seven friends and forty-three sightseers who had come to the great man's farewell. He didn't like funerals. For a man in Steed's dangerous calling it doesn't do to invite introspection. The idea of dying might become too real. He decided to do some of those abdominal exercises in the mornings.

"When S.H. became Home Secretary more than a decade ago he was fittingly known as the Iron Man, and I think we should try to remember him as he then was . . ."

It was a singularly uninteresting church anyway. A pre-Raphaelite Jesus set the tone of precious insensitivity by the font, the stained glass windows would have made a Pepsi Cola bottle look original and the wrought iron round the altar was imitation-Tijou, done by a nineteenth-century blacksmith after a quick visit to Hampton Court. There were too many churches in London that had been built simply to pack in the surplus masses after the industrial revolution had caused a spirtual crisis.

"The Prime Minister has recorded this touching tribute . . ."

The seven friends were appropriately philistine. They were three journalists, a stout man from the Russian Embassy, a thin man from M.I.5., and a dubious looking character with a bald head. Steed didn't like the look of him; there was an unhealthy glow of perspiration on his white scalp. And the woman in the back pew was Miss Petrova, a heroine of the popular press since she had defected to the west twelve months ago.

When the hymn singing started Steed ambled out into the churchyard. The funeral oration had only made him even more bewildered that Smeck-Hudson had committed suicide. The silly ass had somehow fallen away from his principles, his idealism had vanished. Sir Arthur had suddenly and for no good reason started playing with big boys. The Russian Embassy didn't send an observer along as a Christian gesture. The late S.H. had been up to something more serious than sowing late oats with a defected Russian, something that had driven him to suicide. But what the devil was it?

It was three weeks since the old man had said to him, "There's a rogue politician straying from the herd, Steed. Lives near you in Westminster Mews. Keep an eye on the feller. He's been going downhill for about a year and now he's in real trouble." So Steed had kept a bewildered eye on the feller.

The churchyard was a silent square in the heart of London, and Steed watched a couple of typists passing a lunch hour in feeding the pigeons with their sandwiches. They were being too generous. No wonder they looked so thin, with matchstick legs protruding from those delightful mini-skirts, like birds. Their footsteps would probably leave cross marks in the snow. The steady noise of the traffic seemed a long way off.

The character with the bald head came out of the

church, mopping his expansive face with a massive white handkerchief. He wasn't the friendly type, and when Steed fell into step beside him he quickened his pace.

"Not a bad day for a burial," Steed murmured chattily.

"That depends whether you're dead or not," said the man. He had a Brooklyn accent.

"You must be an American cousin," said Steed.

The face registered large suspicion and he denied being related to anybody. "I went inside out of curiosity."

Steed nodded. "Some people can never resist a funeral. I had a relative who was the same, she used to attend funerals for people she had never met. Did you know the Iron Man?"

"I never heard of him." The American waddled into the swarming street and was lost among the hungry office workers. But Steed was confident of improving their acquaintance later.

Tamara Petrova passed on her way home. She looked like the sort of nurse that television serials invented, but who was in fact a doctor. When she came to England it was hailed as a brain drain, only she was the first and last. She was a brain surgeon, now ostensibly unemployed.

Steed waited outside the churchyard in his custom-built pre-war Bentley until the rest of the mourners emerged. He was almost convinced that his job was over; you can't keep an eye on a man who is dead; but from force of habit he decided to find out a little more of what his job had been. Steed leaned over the window and raised his hat. "Can I give you a lift?" he asked as Fletcher, the M.I.5. man strutted past.

Fletcher stopped abruptly. "Good Lord. Steed! Fancy seeing you in this tank. I suppose it's bullet proof. Ha ha." He banged the coachwork experimentally and then climbed up into the seat. "Where's the man who walks in front with the flag? Ha ha."

It was part of Steed's job to be pleasant with people like Fletcher, so he drawled something about giving the chap the day off to go to his grandmother's funeral. Fletcher brayed again. Fletcher was the kind of draft-fodder that had been put into Military Intelligence because he lacked the physique for commando training. The army still thought that non-athletic types must be bright. Of course, Steed had been in Militiary Intelligence during the whatsit, but that only proved that the army makes mistakes.

"Bloody boring funeral," Fletcher groaned. "Takes a lot more than wind to make Smeck-Hudson seem a loss to the species. Bloody old stuffed apricot."

Steed nodded. "But I gather he went downhill a bit during the last twelve months."

"Yes. Maybe he was human. Some people reach adolescence when they're fifty-five."

"They don't often run foul of M.I.5 at that age," Steed said, as casual conversation. "I suppose it wouldn't be diplomatic to ask you what he did."

Fletcher slapped the wooden panel of the door a couple of times to show that he was "flummoxed". Then he said that Smeck-Hudson hadn't done anything. "Not that we know of, apart from gad about with that Russian doctor. Didn't that strike you as odd? I mean, she can't have *liked* him, can she? What was it all about?"

"Some women are easily impressed. I expect he told her what a great Home Secretary he was."

"Good lord, I hope not!"

Fletcher clearly had no idea what he was expected to see at the funeral, or if he did know anything he was cleverly revealing nothing. Steed listened to him for a while, agreed that it was a gay life being a man about town and said that he had never felt the lure of a steady job. The fact that he did have gainful employment Steed didn't like to mention; a gentleman doesn't discuss his business. He dropped Fletcher off at King's Cross.

"By the way," said Fletcher as he closed the door, "I gather you've done a few jobs in this undercover lark."

"Oh, nothing much," Steed said airily. "I was able to help once or twice. Let me know if there's anything you can't handle."

Fletcher smiled. "We seem to have everything under control at the moment. But it was nice to know that you cared."

It was an affront to his professional dignity, and Steed drove all the way back to Westminster with flashy expertise, changing up and down the gearbox with the smooth panache of Sir John Cobb. He hooted the ancient two-note hooter as he passed the Houses of Parliament and chuckled at a Jaguar that stalled by St. James' Park. A man and his machine.

He wouldn't have been so sensitive if he had known that Smeck-Hudson was merely a has-been who had had it, or if he knew that he had been working for the Russians, or compromised. But to be warned off a tantalising mystery was too much. Steed decided to have another look in the dead man's flat.

"Good afternoon," Steed called to the doorman. "January weather we're having!" He waved his umbrella and strode up the stairs to the second floor. The porter said it was parky and made a gesture suspiciously like tugging his forelock; he didn't interfere.

A sliver of perspex down the side of the lock and a sharp push. Steed let himself into the flat as if he owned it. He always assumed that burglars get caught because they look like criminals. He hummed a few bars of the prelude to Lohengrin as he leaned back against the door. Now came the tedious part of searching systematically through the drawers and mattresses and suit linings. He wondered whether to turn on the radio, but that would be tempting providence and it was Woman's Hour.

Half an hour later he sat on the single bed and examined all his sad discoveries. Sir Arthur Smeck-Hudson had been an inveterate collector of trivia, old letters about nothing and old bills, bus tickets, and holiday snapshots, the documentation of an honest life. But there was also conclusive proof that he had been broke, and that something like a hundred thousand pounds had been spent in his last year.

That isn't the sort of money that you can drink away. It takes a deliberate effort on somebody's part.

You can't even spend it on a woman and obtain more than you could get for a mink coat. It had clearly been gambled away . . . and that was legal in swinging London.

It was such a dourly impersonal flat, all oak panelling and antique furniture, heavy oil paintings and thick carpet, the sort of things that money can buy. It felt like a solicitor's office. Steed wished that there was just one etching of the Zulu War on the wall, a postcard on the bathroom door saying 'This is It' or a copy of *Fanny Hill* among the books. There's more to the printed word than *The History of the English Speaking Peoples*. Even *Mein Kampf* would give balance. S.H. hadn't gone downhill in the right direction. His cocktail cabinet contained only whisky, and that a non-proprietary brand.

Steed sipped carefully at a large Scotch on the rocks. The fellow had drunk without aesthetic refinement. As he had dressed with a puritanical intent to conceal his body. And eaten to keep body and soul together. In the Smeck-Hudson kitchen Steed had found a bottle of sauce. The man was just not likeable.

Tamara Petrova had not been attracted to the man unless she was a very odd woman.

Steed was interrupted in his reflections on the vagaries of woman by a scratching at the door. Somebody was fiddling at it with skeleton keys. Steed picked up the more recent souvenirs of this club and that pub, various bills and slipped them into his pocket. Then he sat in a comfortable winged armchair and waited for the visitor.

The visitor was the American cousin.

"You should have rung," said Steed, "I would have opened the door."

The American cousin became melodramatic in his embarrassment and started waving a gun about. Get over there and put your hands up. As if this were the St. Valentine's Day massacre on a smaller scale. Steed tried to be friendly, but it didn't work. He even volunteered to go, leaving the flat free for the cousin to ransack, but that didn't answer the man's needs. And then a commotion started in the passage outside and people kept banging on the door.

This threw the American cousin; he rushed over to the door and stood there as if his physical presence would solve the problem. Then he blundered across to the window and Steed used the crook of his umbrella to trip the fellow up. The next few moves happened rapidly. Steed swung the umbrella round and pressed a catch in the handle; a narrow blade slipped out from the shaft and rested delicately on the man's throat.

"Don't bother to pick up the gun," said Steed. "Just stand up slowly and then open the door. It sounds as if somebody wants to come in."

"They'll ask you questions as well," growled the man.

"I doubt it."

When the porter came in Steed gave him the gun and told him to watch the American. Then he sent the cleaner off to phone the police and went outside to assure the sightseers that nothing had happened,

go back into your flats. He was gone by the time the
police arrived.

"Something going on upstairs," Steed called. "I
think they need you."

The commissionaire went off to investigate. Steed
whistled a casual air, paused on the steps to adjust
the angle of his bowler, and then strolled down to his
car.

There was a large florid man in chauffeur's uniform
at the wheel.

"Get in, Mr. Steed. I'll take you for a ride."

"I don't like people driving my Bentley." It sounded prim, but Steed was like that; he was fussy about
toothbrushes as well; and women. "What's all this
about?" He objected to the man's moustache as well.

"His Nibs wants to see you." The chauffeur leaned
across and opened the nearside door for Steed. "He
wants you to join him for afternoon tea."

"He could always drop me an invitation . . ."

Steed sighed fatalistically and sat beside Benson.
The man drove as if he thought the car was a joke.
"You ought to save up, Mr. S., and buy yourself a
little Volkswagen for Christmas." Benson had been
the traditional cockney batman during the war, keeping the officers laughing from Cairo to Tobruk with
reminiscences of the Mile End Road, and when the
misunderstanding had been cleared up Benson had remained with His Nibs still serving him with prole-
tarian devotion. It was a sentimental tale. "Don't look
so worried, Mr. S. You'll soon be noshing it up in

those posh tearooms while I'm next door in the working man's caff."

"Hard luck!"

To Steed's horror they drew up outside one of those tea shops in Knightsbridge where the keynote is gentility. But it looked as if they had taken down the Christmas decorations. And with any luck the woman who owned the place would still be in Tunbridge Wells with her family.

"I'll stay here, Mr. S. in case the law tries to tow the scrap metal away."

It isn't easy to be nonchalant under such circumstances. Steed glanced around and then slipped furtively into the tearooms. Fragile furniture aspiring to the eighteenth century and a horsey waitress. The single room that looked like a room was crowded with women who'd been to the Harrods sale. And a military cove in the corner.

"Steed, my boy, come and sit down! Glad you could make it. Have you tried the scrambled egg on toast here?"

He took a few moments to hang up his bowler. "Er—no, actually. I prefer—"

"You'll enjoy it. Eggs are a meal in themselves!"

Steed muttered something about happiness being scrambled.

"They make a good pot of tea as well. Waitress! Your trouble is, my lad, that you don't eat the proper food. Just taste this tea."

Steed sipped it carefully and then nodded. "I believe they offer a dividend as well?"

"Eh? Oh, I see." He frowned. "All right, please

yourself. Order what you like, and don't blame me when you waste away to nothing."

"I won't, sir." He beamed charmingly and ordered a glass of lemon tea. "China, of course."

The retired major-general glowered unhappily. "I suppose that funeral put you off your appetite, eh? Depressing things, funerals. Still, as long as you've got to the bottom of this business. . . ."

Steed had to admit that he was nowhere near the bottom. "I'm not even sure that Smeck-Hudson had been passing information to the Russians. He was compromised, of course, but he may have committed suicide rather than betray his country. He seems to have been that sort of man."

"He was a fool, letting himself go downhill like that," snapped the old man. "He should have known there are people—organised people who will take advantage of a public figure who lets himself go. Why did he do it?"

Steed shrugged his shoulders. He may have been disillusioned with his career; he was a most unpopular Home Secretary. But it was courting trouble to mention psychology to the military mind. Retired major-generals don't understand what loneliness and self pity can do to a rich but unattractive man. "Perhaps," said Steed, "he became involved with the wrong woman."

"You're a romantic, Steed. But Smeck-Hudson wasn't. I met the fellow when he was on the way up and I understood him then. It would have taken something pretty terrible to bring this about."

Steed lit a small imported panatella and puffed at

it for several seconds. "You suspect something like brainwashing, sir?"

"I don't suspect anything. I'll wait for you to discover the facts."

"I don't think he passed on any information," said Steed. "I was passing the time of day with Fletcher after the funeral—."

"I know, M.I.5 have declared themselves satisfied. No further action to be taken. I know." The old man smiled rather chillingly and took a newspaper from his brief case. He was no longer an old buffer playing a game. "Have you seen this?"

"No, it looks like Pravda and my Russian is shaky—"

"There's an obituary. They claim that Smeck-Hudson was an affectionist and they claim that his last information to them was a detailed report on the Regional Seats of Government which are set up in this country for use after a nuclear attack. As far as I can see the details are absolutely authentic."

"I see."

"You were meant to be keeping an eye on him."

"I'm sorry, sir, but Smeck-Hudson would have known about the R.S.G.s since he was Home Secretary. They were established in the late 1950s, weren't they?" You couldn't admit you were wrong to the old man, otherwise you'd be eating scrambled eggs at all hours of the day. "I still find it difficult to believe."

"It's an organised group with methods for achieving the difficult things and they'll go on doing them until this country is ruined."

Steed sipped his lemon tea thoughtfully. "I wonder whom they'll choose next."

"You."

Steed shuddered. It was the cold weather. "I'm sure you know what you're doing, sir." He prodded the slice of lemon. "Do we know much about this organisation?"

His Nibs beamed encouragingly. "Nothing at all. Although the Petrova woman is the obvious way in. You'll have to go through the whole process. . . ."

"They don't pick on just anybody—"

"They seem to be mainly interested in propaganda value rather than state secrets. That information about the R.S.G.s for instance isn't nearly as important as the fact that they got it from an ex-Home Secretary. The Russians love a lord or an M.P. So you'll have to be transparently corruptible, and we'll need to arrange your future."

Steed smiled. "I knew my record would be noticed sooner or later. Lord Steed, eh? My mother would be very proud."

"You'll be an M.P. and like it," said the ex-soldier. "I'm only a bloody sir myself!"

The will to power had never been very strong in Steed, and his respect for politicians had been circumscribed. "Does that mean I'll have to stand for parliament?"

"Of course it does."

"For which party?"

"Good lord, Steed, don't be so bloody flippant! What does it matter which party? You'll stand for

Smeck-Hudson's old constituency. It's a safe seat. You're not a liberal or anything, are you?"

"Good lord no, sir."

3

"What do you think about hanging, Mr. Steed?"

"It must be a very unpleasant experience."

The adoption committee had been distinctly chilly. They obviously resented having a candidate thrust upon them by the party executive. A constituency party has the right to choose its own candidate, and a central directive is usually enough to ruin a man's chances of selection. But Steed had been chosen by the five stalwarts of Brawhill because the Chairman was nobbled and two more had been women.

"What is your attitude towards immigration, Mr. Steed?"

Steed had smiled blandly and admitted that it can lead to difficulties. "I know that an ancestor of mine took great exception to the way the Normans came over here and disrupted the life of the country. Robin Hood—you may have heard of him. But he was proved wrong by history and the Sheriff of Not-

tingham's crowd was eventually absorbed quite suc-
cessfully."

An intense schoolmistress had found that a fascinating analogy. "And what do you think about teenagers?"

"When you reach my age, madam, you only envy
them." This had gone down rather well because the
old thing was past middle age. Steed had dealt with
roads, education ("I didn't enjoy it myself but I suppose childhood isn't all innocent fun"), housing and
the war against crime. And the committee had gradually responded to him, deceived by the casual air of
authority into thinking that he would cut a fine figure
in the House of Commons and so reflect credit on
them. "I find the suppressed hysteria of ordinary
citizens far more alarming than most of the problems
they get hysterical about," Steed sighed.

The only difficult one was an unsuccessful barrister who obviously had his own ambitions for a career
in Westminster. He had carefully placed his wristwatch on the table and asked Steed to make a fifteen
minute speech outlining his ideas to reassure those
hysterical floating voters. That had appeared to be
the standard procedure.

"I would have made some notes," Steed had said.
Then he had taken the Hunter from his fob pocket
and placed it carefully beside the wristwatch while
he had wondered how hard he could slap down
the pompous young man without alienating the rest
of the committee.

"A particular candidate," the barrister had per-
sisted, "can affect about five per cent of the vote."

"The only way to keep everybody happy," Steed had said solemnly, "would be to set aside an area like Wales for those people who want to live the tough way. They could hang and flog each other, persecute minorities and conscript teenagers into the Welsh Foreign Legion. They could have a wonderful time, building roads and skyscrapers and abolishing free medical treatment—"

"Wouldn't that be rather hard on the Welsh?"

"I'm sure they'd want to come back to England. It would be such a pleasant place to live without that element."

"But what about politics?" the barrister had asked.

"They wouldn't be very important, would they?" Steed had given them all a radiant smile, returned his watch to his pocket, picked up his curly rimmed bowler and saluted with his umbrella. "Shall I wait outside while you deliberate?" At the door he had turned back. "Oh by the way," he had added as an afterthought, "my only real disadvantage is that I'm not awfully good with babies. But I'm charming with their mothers."

The occasion had ended in great triumph. It transpired that the barrister was disliked by the rest of the committee and they felt that he had been put down. And afterwards in the pub across the road Steed had impressed them all with his political awareness by telling them about Lloyd George and the occasions between the wars when the great man had stayed with his father for weekends. They hadn't minded that L.G. was a Liberal.

Nevertheless Steed was relieved to be back in London. The industrial Midlands was a depressing place, a memorial to greed and man's inhumanity to man, unrelieved by the monumental breweries and the endless stretches of back to back houses where the people bred their social problems. Steed found to his dismay that the place brought out a moralistic streak in him. King's Cross was an easier place to detest with a light heart.

He hailed a taxi and gave the driver an address in Pimlico.

It was half past twelve at night, but Steed was following in the path of a man who had burnt the candle through till morning—like a child, he reflected, afraid of the dark. The continuous round of clubs and pubs that Steed had been following these last few days had kept him out of bed until five every morning, and a few hours in Brawhill was no excuse for an early night.

The Mississippi was the shadiest gambling joint of the whole lot, where the most unpleasant people played for the highest stakes. But it was luxurious, to encourage lavishness. It was a boat on the Thames done out like an American river boat; the steam engine didn't work and the magnificent paddle-wheels never turned, but the ornamentation was genuine and the staterooms (named after American states) were quite authentic. The only gesture to current fashion was the anachronism of the staff's costume—they were dressed as cowboys and cowgirls. But the gamblers didn't mind.

Steed sighed as he prepared to leave the taxi. He prided himself on knowing spirits, holding his liquor and being a gentleman at all times. But the course of duty overrides even the ten commandments. Steed staggered from the cab, laughed inanely and slurred his speech as he told the driver to keep the change. Then he lurched up the gangplank and waved Smeck-Hudson's membership card at a man who looked like Lee Marvin.

"Hey you, Jesse James," he guffawed, "is that gun loaded?" It was a serious question, but he decided that when he left the House of Commons it would be for the House of Lords or nothing. "Bang, bang, what?" He tapped it playfully and found that it was for show.

"Straight through, buddy. The fists are genuine."

Steed had another argument with the cloak room girl, who wanted to take his umbrella. He pretended that he didn't want any petrol, then he launched into a routine about not being able to tell the men from the women now that you fellers are wearing your hair so long ("And what instrument do you play?") and finally he confessed that he had a brandy flask concealed in the handle.

He kept his umbrella and went down into the main saloon. There was something delectable about so many girls in tight riding trousers, studded belts and wearing spurs. Unless supposing all gamblers weren't masochists? Steed glanced at the roulette wheel and then made a detour of the room, examining the customers and fixing the geography of the place in his mind. It was his second visit and he had to get down to work.

There were ten people sitting absorbed at the

roulette table, listening to the pigeon French of the croupier and pushing their chips in silence onto the squares, watching the wheel hypnotically, and the cigarette smoke proved they were breathing. The same scene exactly as Monte Carlo or Las Vegas or Hong Kong, the same people. Overweight men with fleshy hands perspiring under the brilliant lights, the skeletons of listless women with deathmask faces, and the young men losing money to prove their manhood. The customarily dubious-looking officials looked even more like outlaws in their wild west drag.

"I don't see Mike O'Hara tonight," Steed said to one of them.

"He isn't here."

"I see that he had a spot of trouble with the police—"

"What's that to you, buddy boy?"

"He's my cousin," said Steed.

The croupier was a girl in her mid-twenties with auburn hair; she knew her job, and part of her job was to appeal to the middle-aged men. She smiled at Steed and nodded towards an empty place. He winked, sat where she instructed and followed the red for seven turns. He lost three hundred and fifty pounds. That was another thing he found embarrassing about this job—it hurt his vanity to have to lose like a fluttering amateur.

"I must say," Steed whispered tipsily to a Buck Jones character, "that croupier knows her stuff. Seat absolutely made for a horse. Does she—?"

"No, she doesn't."

"Shame. I'm going down to the hunt at Barton this weekend—"

"Are you playing?"

"No, drinking, actually."

"You could do with a turn on deck to sober up, buddy boy," said a drawling voice behind him. "Help me up with him, Schlesinger."

Steed was aided unobtrusively but fast up the stairs and out of the saloon, with a pantomime gunman hustling him on each side. There was nothing obvious that he could object to, except for the cold weather blasting along the river. It wasn't the sort of occasion to admire the lights in the distance from Battersea Power Station and the rest of the deck seemed to be deserted. Steed allowed himself to be taken down to the lower deck, and there they waited while a sinisterly large shadow loomed towards them behind the glow of a cigar.

"What's going on, gentlemen?"

"He was asking after Mike, and then we found him poking around."

The man with the cigar spoke with a velvet softness, as casually and as American as a twenty stone James Stewart. "Mr. Steed," he drawled, "I must admit that you worry me. You came in here drunk two nights ago and you lost five hundred pounds. Now you give a repeat performance and you start asking questions as well. I ask myself what will you do at the next performance, and do you know what I answer myself? I tell myself that John Steed is a suspicious character. I tell myself that you come in here on a dead man's membership card, you lose money and yet who are you? where does your money come from? What do you say to that, Mr. Steed?"

Steed hiccupped gently. "I'd say you were a very nervous man. Do you take this interest in all your customers?"

"We have to be careful. Running a gambling joint in London is a nerve-racking business."

"Mainly, it seems, for the customers."

The American stared at him for a long half minute. "Why did you ask after Mike O'Hara?"

Steed laughed inebriately and sat on a safety belt that had S.S. Mississippi painted in illuminated lettering round it. "It's funny you should ask me that. He was an American as well—like you, a jolly suspicious sort of fellow. Do you know, I last met him at poor dead Bongo Hudson's nest, and he behaved in the most extraordinary way. Flourished a gun and all that. Fancy a sniff of brandy?" Steed unscrewed the handle of his umbrella and offered them a drink, but they refused. "Well," he continued refreshed, "your friend Mike was so noisy that the neighbours called the police. I mean, they're a very select class of people in Westminster. You can't behave as you would in Chicago, you know."

The fat man was icily calm, and Steed noticed with surprise that his lack of the fancy dress made him look all the more dangerous. "What," he asked, "were you doing in Smeck-Hudson's flat?"

"What, old Bongo—?"

"Stop clowning and answer the question!"

"He was my friend," Steed said simply. "I'm taking

over from him in the House, you know. M.P. and all that."

The man nodded to himself and then thoughtfully dropped his cigar into the black water below the boat. "I don't want to see you again, Mr. Steed. Ever. And if I catch you interfering in things that don't concern you I'll cut off your hands at the wrists."

The fat man turned silently and walked back into the darkness. He walked gracefully and lightly for a man of his bulk. Steed decided that he was a very dangerous enemy, and events were soon to prove him right.

4

"Mrs. Peel," he said as he opened the door, "we're needed."

"I know. I think I'm psychic." Emma Peel followed him up the flight of stairs to the main part of the mews flat. "As soon as you rang me I said to myself—the old seducer is at it again. He'll weaken my resistance with an exotic meal, lull my suspicions with sweet wine and then send me into the jaws of death."

"Champagne, my dear. I don't allow sweet wine

in the flat, except for cooking purposes. And while we're still being pleasant to each other, you look quite stunning."

Emma smiled graciously and gave him her black fur coat. It was a complete justification of winter. Underneath she was wearing a purple wool boucle jacket and dress that fitted elegantly over the slim curves of her body. The white boots made the cold weather seem desirable as well. But the elaborately feminine aura was dispelled as she sniffed delightedly and said, "Whatever you're cooking, Steed, it smells marvellous! I've decided I'm hungry."

She threw herself onto the sofa, tossed her boots into a corner and curled her feet up under her like an expensive, auburn haired panther. Steed sighed as he poured two aperitifs. It was fortunate that the one real ethic of their profession was never to fall in love. But perhaps when they were both very old, and living in retirement, he might rise up from his wheelchair and leap on Emma. She was twenty-eight now, a widow whose husband had been killed when the jet he was testing had disintegrated, and she lived in modest luxury on the fortune that her father had left her. Emma Peel's only indulgence was a taste for danger, and Steed sometimes suspected that that was only because she thought he wasn't capable of looking after himself.

"I'm going to become an M.P." he murmured casually.

"Have you been drinking all the afternoon?"

"Certainly not," he said indignantly.

Emma collapsed in unseemly laughter. After sev-

eral seconds she spluttered apologies, put down her
glass and carried on laughing.

"Women," Steed said steadily, "are for admiring
gasps and cooing admiration; they are not for guffaws
of satirical laughter."

"I'm sorry, Steed, I'm sure you'll make a wonderful M.P."

"I shall nurse my wounded pride in the kitchen."

Even while he was adding a little more white wine
to the lemon sauce and using it to baste the fowl in
the oven Steed heard a couple of suppressed snorts
from the lounge. He thrust the affront from his mind
while he concentrated on mixing the cream cheese
with the horseradish to fill the halves of unpeeled
apricots.

"Damn!"

"What's the matter?" Emma asked anxiously. "Oh
dear, you've cut your hand on the tin opener."

"I thought it was something like that," said Steed.

"Shall I carry on while you find a bandage?"

"No. In my home a woman's place is *not* in the
kitchen. Wait in the living room for the experience
of a gourmet's lifetime. You wouldn't know how to
carry on this capon with lemons."

Emma returned obediently, taking the *Good Hus-
wives Handmaid* with her. It was published in 1597
and Steed was sentimentally using the recipe to
remind himself of his Elizabethan cottage in Wiltshire
as he hadn't seen it since before Christmas. And it
succeeded; by the time they began the meal Steed's
good humour was restored and Emma was suitably
admiring again.

"I'm replacing Smeck-Hudson," he explained, "so that the people who killed him can have a go at killing me." He sketched in the details of the last few days.

"What I don't understand," Emma said eventually, "is how an American gambling club comes into this Russian plot."

"Neither do I. The owner is a twenty stone thug with a bald head called Curt Krystal. We're trying to get his record from America, assuming he has one. However, I'm handing the Mississippi angle over to you."

Emma smiled ironically. "You don't think he'll cut off my hands?"

"Good lord no! Is this wine to your taste? It's a fifty-nine, of course, but I came cross a dubious bottle last Thursday."

"How distressing," Emma said tartly. "You were telling me. . . ."

"Oh yes. The idea came to me last night while I was remarking on the weather to one of the hostesses. I thought how dashing you would look in one of those cowboy outfits. Mm, a little too dry, perhaps? No—no, perfect. Of course the flappy things on the legs might look odd on you, but think what fun you could have with the lasso."

"You don't suppose I'll look as if I'm selling petrol?"

Steed laughed delightedly. "That's exactly what I said! They were very amused." He got up from the table and gestured Emma to the Regency chair by the fire. It was time to relax after the serious business of eating. "Brandy? Panatella? I'd look after

Krystal myself, but I've been blundering about these last few days expressly to draw attention to myself. You'll have to be the one who slips quietly into their lives from abroad. They must never suspect that you're planted."

A patient lift of the eyebrow. "What's this about abroad?"

"Oh yes, it nearly slipped my mind. You've been enrolled at L'ecole des Croupiers in Monte Carlo. Mr. Krystal always takes his girls from there when he needs one."

"And he'll need one pretty soon," Emma said heavily.

"Exactly."

The whole street was derelict. A few of the houses at one end had been razed to the ground and the rest had been left to rot. Their windows had been smashed, the fences broken down and the squalid gardens cluttered with rubble. At ten thirty in the evening it was an eerie place to stray into and very few people did. The darkness was total, and Steed felt that he was in a ghost town years after the holocaust. Every sound was magnified, the scuttling of a swarm of rats, the hollow pounding of his own footsteps and the furtive shift of an occasional meths man.

Half-way along the street Steed paused, and then went into the shell of a house. He wondered how people managed to carry baths and car wreckage into these gardens. He wondered why the smell of derelict humanity was always like an untended lavatory, as if the sewer were the symbol of society.

Steed tried to close the shattered front door, and gave up when he realised that he was disturbing a creature on the floor of the hallway. An aged or young ruin of a man, unshaven, muttering to himself, with bright insane eyes that forced you to recognise how far a man can be pushed into other worlds. Steed held his breath and went on up the stairs.

There were another half dozen of these meths men before he reached the top floor. But they ignored him, oblivious to anything but their constant search for crude spirit; they didn't even talk to each other. They would only be touched now by death.

Arthur Thorburn had looked dissipated when his favourite drink was still ginger beer; he had found that the romantically tubercular look went down well with girls. He was the obvious man for the job. Now his clothes were suitably tattered rags and his beard was seemingly alive with lice. He glanced up lethargically from his corner as Steed came in.

"I was beginning to think you weren't coming."

"Sorry, old sport, but I had to put a lady on a plane to Monte. Don't tell me you people are bothered by time."

Steed stepped carefully across the floor of the bare room and looked out of the window. He could see the lights of the good ship Mississippi fifty yards away. "What's been going on then?" he asked. He took the binoculars from Thorburn and peered at the portholes.

"You can't see inside," said Thorburn. "The windows mist up in this weather. I've kept a list of all the comings and goings. Madame Petrova is in there now."

"Is she indeed?" Steed whistled silently. "Who was she with?"

"A little fellow; I didn't recognise him. When they come out I'll snap him with the infra red. We'll soon trace him."

Steed nodded, put the list in his pocket and passed appropriate remarks about the time of year. "How is it those creatures on the stairs don't die of pneumonia?" he asked.

"They do."

"Oh well, look after yourself."

Thorburn snorted ungraciously; his work was getting him down. "Incidentally, I found out who the croupier is. French girl called Annette Lantier, and her visa expires next week."

"Clever old chap. Make sure it isn't renewed, won't you? Just in case I forget to mention it. Well, good night."

Steed went back downstairs. On the first landing he tripped on a meths man who screamed hideously and tried to fight him. Steed pushed him gently away. The man was weak as a baby, and he relapsed into his private nightmare.

"I think we are in rats' alley," Steed murmured to himself, "where dead men drag their bones." But Eliot hadn't known the half of it.

Steed returned into the fresh air feeling somewhat depressed. He glanced bleakly at the notice at the end of the street which jocularly announced a new housing estate on the site, "which would include a restaurant, child care centre and double car park." No place then for rats, or men who hadn't asked to be born and didn't want to be kept alive.

The laughter and music from the Mississippi sounded discordant. Steed walked further along the embankment and waited, gazing into the Thames. He liked the Thames. Lechlade, Windsor, the Festival Hall and the old fishing village of Leigh; the river passed through a comforting span of English life. He liked the way the light dispersed in the water, shimmering in the icy black currents. What a shame it didn't freeze over any more, for the public roasting of an ox and supper on skates. Although that would be a disaster to shipping and ruin Britain's balance of payments.

Steed lit a panatella and watched a bad tempered couple emerge from the gambling boat. They had seemingly lost when the woman had been on a winning streak, and only Curt Krystal was laughing. Someone had fallen, the man said, and changed the whole course of their fate. "They should have picked him up and thrown him overboard!"

A church clock nearby struck eleven, and while it was striking Big Ben began and a few seconds later another joined in, clocks from all directions in a symphony of electronic music, and the roar of motor cars, the occasional hoot of a horn made it unmistakeably Stockhausen's idea of London. Steed realised with surprise how noisy the evening was.

There were voices raised from the Mississippi and Steed saw the silhouette of a man being helped down the gangplank. The woman helping him was Tamara Petrova. One or both of them was in a state of agitation, and probably the man was trying to release himself from her. Steed threw his panatella into the river and ambled across to his Bentley. The man was now standing by the kerb and waving unsteadily for a taxi.

Steed had to leap aside suddenly to avoid a wild Morris Oxford that shot round from a side street. He caught a glimpse of the driver's crumpled face, like a boxer's complete with broken nose and cauliflower ears. And while he was still muttering to himself about maniacs-at-the-wheel a screeching of brakes and a sickening crunch of metal against metal made his stomach heave. A woman's scream cut through the air and then people began rushing from all directions to stare at the man grovelling in the road.

"He was drunk!" shouted a man who had been standing on the gangplank of the Mississippi. "He staggered into the road."

"Murderer!" Tamara Petrova shouted after the receding car. "Stop! You've killed him!"

But the car didn't stop, and the argument on the pavement reached a rapid pitch of hysteria, as if any activity was better than just watching the man in the gutter bleed to death. There was nothing that Steed could add to the situation, so he drove off as soon as the police arrived.

Emma Peel read the news of Cyril Maxton's death in the airmail edition of the *Daily Telegraph* next morning. He was a minor official in the Home Office, aged 47, a bachelor, and worth a paragraph as a news item. Emma carried on nibbling her croissant while she concentrated on the serious problem of what to wear for the Mediterranean winter. She had hoped it would be warm enough to skip the first morning's classes and go for a swim, but even Monte Carlo is less exotic in the winter than a summer's day. She decided that duty must prevail.

In the continental papers she found a more speculative account of Maxton's death, linking it to Smeck-Hudson's suicide. These mysterious cases of high-up degeneracy and death, one waffled in gleeful French, are regarded in some quarters as further evidence of British decadence, but official circles suspect a ring of clever foreign helpers who are shepherding the foolish to disaster. Some of the very top undercover agents are working on the theory. . . .

Well, it was nice to know that her top status was acknowledged. She selected a black shark-skin blouse to go with the tight black trousers and tossed the rest of the croissant into the coffee. It was the sort of weather that made an English girl insular.

5

Steed paused half-way up the front path and picked a winter rose for his buttonhole. Nothing like a flower to impress the opposite sex. Then he twirled his umbrella in a complex action that ended by his prodding the doorbell. He was calling to pay respects to a strange lady for the first time in twenty odd years. It was positively rejuvenating. He stepped back and viewed the rambling Victorian house with approval; he liked those interesting corners, weird towers and sudden jutting walls.

The lace curtains moved in the front bay window. But nobody answered the door. After a few seconds Steed stepped across the lawn and peered into the window. He could hear an odd whirring noise that interested him.

"Yes?" a woman's voice demanded behind him.

"Hello," Steed said with a tip of his bowler. "You're Madame Petrova."

"I know." The woman was large-boned and blonde; described by the popular press as a Ukranian beauty, but she was the sort of heroine that you see romping romantically in Russian films, bouncing about on beds with the young hero and punching him playfully about the body, so that you become extremely worried about the punishment the hero is taking. On closer inspection she might be almost forty, and tough. "What do you want?"

"I'm John Steed. You might have heard of me. I thought I'd drift round and leave my card."

Tamara was baffled. "To leave what?"

"My card. You know, it's an old English custom. This is my card." He produced a visiting card like a conjuror and flipped it triumphantly into her palm. "That establishes our friendship, you see. It's symbolic."

"Of what?" Tamara scrutinised the card, glanced at Steed and then looked back to the card. "It doesn't say what you do."

"Good lord, I don't do anything. Ha. ha. Good lord no."

"You just go around leaving your card with people . . ."

Steed laughed good humouredly. "Well, no, as a matter of fact I am doing something now. I'm Smeck-Hudson's successor. We all have to start being useful sooner or later. So I thought, as S.H.'s successor I'd drift round and commiserate with poor old Madame Petrova. It's the thing to do you know in England."

"And what do people in England do when people do that?"

"Oh, they usually ask the chap in for a stiff brandy. By the time he's been through the explanations he usually needs one."

Madame Petrova smiled. "Come in and have a brandy."

"Very courteous of you." Steed was beginning to understand how that character in *Ninotchka* felt when he tried to get through to Greta Garbo. Some women are just not susceptible. He followed her into a chintzy reception room that had more lace curtains and one of those heavy oak sideboards. The potted plants looked like mandrakes. "You're gone native, I see," said Steed.

"In what sense do you mean you are Sir Arthur's successor?"

For a hideous moment Steed thought she was being frisky. "Oh, in the House of Commons, that's all. I've been adopted as parliamentary candidate for Brawhill."

"I see." With superb literal-mindedness Tamara handed him a brandy and stood there to watch him drink it. It didn't seem as if he was intended to stay for long.

"Cheers. Yes, it was very sad about S.H. He must have been pushed pretty hard to kill himself like that. And a nasty shock for you, eh?"

"I hadn't seen him for three weeks. I grew tired of his constant self pity. He was not an attractive man."

"He was unattractive when you met him." Steed prowled across the room, glanced out of the window, examined the books and admired the pictures while Tamara grew agitated. Steed decided that she deserved all the tension he could create for her; any woman who actually liked that Landseer family group was in need of treatment. He tapped a concealed microphone by the glass dome of flowers, and traced the lead to a tape recorder among the bottom bookshelves. It was not switched on.

"I see from the newspapers that you lost another sparring partner last night," he said casually. "You should have read your horoscope before embarking on a new romance this month. After all, it looks so bad. Did you know that *Figaro* is speculating on whether you're a Russian spy?"

"I never read French newspapers." Tamara was really becoming nervous, uncertain how much of a buffoon this English gentleman could be taken for. "If I were still in touch with Russia I should not be so open in my associations."

"Yes, that occurred to me." Steed relaxed on the chaise longue. "Is that vague whirr I hear the grind of a generator? But I mustn't ask too many questions. My apologies. It's just that one forgets that a beautiful woman is also a research scientist. Do you have much chance to keep up to date in this country?"

"I keep my hand in. You must meet my assistants." Tamara smiled frostily, and pressed the service button by the mantelpiece. "So many people take an interest in me that I need what you might call protection."

The door opened and Tamara's three assistants came in. They were women. Steed rose to his feet and bowed to the three Chinese girls in their white silk judo-gi outfits. They bowed back, but they didn't say anything. Neither did they smile. Steed declared himself enchanted and wondered how many ghastly weapons they could conceal in those loose-fitting robes. He decided not to find out. Mrs. Peel could no doubt deal with them if it came to the point. A gentleman never fights with women.

"Aren't they pretty?" Tamara demanded.

"Exquisite," he said truthfully.

They were like Dresden figurines, and probably they appealed to Madame Petrova's love of Victoriana. Steed waited to see whether they would launch into a quick chorus of 'Three Little Maids' or put on a display of the seven basic throws. In fact they sat on the floor and stared inscrutably at him for the rest of his visit.

"I don't suppose," Steed said to be sociable, "that they get much exercise here in London."

"They have special methods for keeping fit."

Yes, they looked well enough. "And how are you finding this country?"

"We like it," Tamara answered.

Steed was about to make the usual remarks about freedom and individual liberty, but it would have sounded silly even for his present pose. How on earth, he wondered, would he survive three weeks of electioneering. "You don't find that the health of the pound worries you?"

"Mr. Steed, I don't understand what you are talking about, and I'd like to know what you've come here for. I was warned about you, and I know that you aren't an idiot. I should like you to tell me what you want."

"I see that I can't fool you," said Steed. "I'm not surprised the Russians were sorry to lose you." He smiled diffidently, and helped himself to another brandy. "I suppose I'm worried about taking over from Smeck-Hudson in the house. In some respects I'd rather not step into his shoes, you see. I'm a coward. So I've spent a couple of evenings reassuring myself about him, in case I was heading for an early death."

Tamara was watching him even more suspiciously, and her fair skin darkened slightly with emotion. She was stroking the hair of one of the Chinese girls, idly, as if she were a kitten. "As we've already discussed, Mr. Steed, why be suspicious of me?"

"For the reasons we've already discussed, Madame Petrova. Did you know that Smeck-Hudson disappeared for two whole weeks just over a year ago? No record at all of where he was; although he was a bachelor so nobody would really have cared. In that fortnight I think he was brainwashed. Not just persuaded that communism was all right or shown the error of America's ways—he wasn't that kind of liberal. He was physically subjected to a mental reconstruction. Which of course is a very painful operation."

"Are you suggesting—?"

"Nothing, old thing. Just a chat between friends. After all, you did ask me. The interesting thing about brainwashing is that it can usually be undone; you know, Smeck-Hudson could have been reconverted to his old, insular belief in the British lion, unless he was strictly controlled during that spectacular year when he was ruining himself."

"And you suppose—?"

"Yes, I think I know how it was done." Steed beamed proudly and offered his feminine audience a panatella while they were enjoying the exposition. To his surprise Tamara accepted one. She was a woman after Tallulah Bankhead's heart. "I think they used lysergic acid to break him during that fortnight. It's an old trick that the Germans used during the war, although you ladies will be too young to remember. It's a drug that reduces a person to helpless addiction and drives him mad when it's withheld. Not really a nice thing to do to a friend."

Tamara was icily indifferent. "Does this concern me?"

"It does rather, because Cyril Maxton was under the influence of lysergic acid when he was killed last night. He wasn't drunk, he was drugged at the time of the murder."

Steed retrieved his umbrella and bowler from the hall, gave the girls a cheery good afternoon, and let himself out of the house. As he ambled down the garden path to the gate he turned with a debonair wave of the hand. He always enjoyed making new friends.

6

When the man tried to kill him Steed was at home reading an improving book. He had thought of going back to search Tamara's house, because something was clearly wrong there. But his sense of duty had triumphed. He hadn't fancied meeting three Chinese women in mortal combat and staying at home had seemed a safer proposition. Westminster Mews was normally such a civilised place.

Steed put Bach's Brandenburg Concerto on the stero record player and situated himself carefully between the loudspeakers. He preferred to sit slightly closer to the harpsichord. Then he drank the first of the three large Napoleon brandies he had promised himself to aid concentration and began to plod his way through *Traffic in Towns*. A solid read, lacking the scope of Tolstoy or the humanity of Dickens, but it was apparently the aspiring politician's manual.

"Planning, that's what it's all about," Steed's agent had assured him. "Whenever a problem is insoluble then you talk about planning and everybody is happy. You know what the English middle-class vote is like. They all want two cars and they want a green and pleasant land. They want *other* people prevented from having cars, but they can't afford to upset General Motors. So gen yourself up on planning, boy."

The agent was a seedy man called Wilson with seven successes in the House so far. He had assured Steed that a candidate only needs to gen himself up on one subject. "That will impress them with your grasp, old boy, so they won't notice you're waffling about defence and hospitals."

"What," Steed had asked in distaste, "are your politics?"

"I've always been too busy to vote, old man. You have the politics and leave me with the practical details, eh? We'll get along that way. And don't, please, tell them you went to Eton. That still impresses the women but Heath and Harold have put across a different image now, of the technocratic government." —

Steed was sipping his second brandy; the fourth concerto was resolving itself magically and the fire was crackling up on to a woozy blaze. He was thinking how pleasant it must have been in eighteenth-century Leipzig, with none of the squalid overspill populations and roadwidening schemes to worry about. Although maybe twenty-one children had upset the tranquillity of Johann Sebastian's evenings. Perhaps a fourth brandy before he retired to bed.

Then the grandfather clock at the top of the stairs began striking, and went on striking. Somebody had found his way into the garage below the flat. Steed sighed and went out onto the landing. He had so few pleasant evenings at home. He flicked off the alarm and waited for the intruder to come up the back stairs. But every job, he supposed, has its disadvantages.

A slight creak announced the man's arrival on the other side of the door. He was turning the handle, slowly, with the infinite stealth of a man without accomplices. Then gradually the door opened. Steed concealed himself behind the grandfather clock just in case the safety system didn't work. Bach was reaching one of his perfect conclusions, in a timeless rebuke to these lapses into human savagery. Then the intruder pushed the door half-way open and the four feet square of floor gave way beneath him. He hung onto the handle as he fell and the gun in his other hand fired into nowhere. Then he landed ten feet below in the tiny room that had once been a kiln when Westminster Mews had been stables.

Steed went back to finish his brandy and hear the final note of the concerto. The prisoner would be quite safe in the kiln until Steed felt like releasing him.

Emma Peel was standing on the deck looking out across the harbour. She felt sad, looking at the moon suspended in the dark blue sky like a captured symbol of the universe. The yellow surface was so yellow and the shadows gave it such an impressive texture. But its days of romance were over and lovers would soon cease staring at the moon in June. There was a rocket whizzing round the thing, and the craters were littered with scientific instruments. What a shame, she thought, to be certain that there is no man in the moon.

"It is an entrancing night, is it not?" The Italian was looking at the yachts which littered the bay, probably listening to the millionaire parties and the sounds of laughter that floated across the calm water; he would be reassured that rich people were so happy. He owned one of the casinos.

"Delightful," said Emma. "Shall we go down and see the man?"

The man was a dishevelled Sicilian who would pass for a peasant in any company. He belched casually as he waved Emma to a chair and then eased his trousers into the chair behind the desk. He had to sit a foot back from the desk to accommodate his stomach. This was Don Mario.

"My cousin owns the Mississippi Club in London," Don Mario explained tersely. "He needs a croupier and you have been recommended to me."

Emma smiled, but it didn't charm Don Mario.

"You have your certificate from L'Ecole?"

Emma passed it across the table.

Don Mario had learned his rude English when the Americans had landed in Sicily in 1944, but he had never learned to read in any language. He gave the certificate to the Italian escort, who read it with appropriate lip movements and handed it back to Emma.

"Do you know why you have been chosen?" he asked.

"No." Dispense with the frills of conversation and stick to the point. "Why have I?"

Don Mario spat the end of his cigar in the general direction of the ash tray. "Because it is almost impossible to check your past, because you cheated in the casino this afternoon, and because this certificate is a forgery. You have only been at L'Ecole one week so this cannot be genuine."

"In short," Emma said nervously, "I'm exactly the kind of girl you need." She wondered what on earth the man had been told about her past. The intended story was that she had been running a club in Deal which was closed down by the police. As for her cheating in the afternoon craps practice, she had been perfecting the blanket roll; someone had been clever to spot it.

"I will send you to my cousin," said Don Mario, "but if he discovers you have fake credentials he will be very angry. You will be washed up by the tide one morning, and that would be painful." He heaved himself to his feet and waddled round to the door. "So you will report some things to me, and then I won't let him know. Good evening, Mrs. Peel."

Steed finished his lunch and then went down the back stairs to the garage. The intruder had been in the kiln for fifteen hours and it was time to find out what there was to find out. The fellow had been well behaved; only one spell of shouting at around breakfast.

"Come out of there," Steed instructed as he opened the small brick door.

Another bullet buried itself in the wall as Steed jumped aside. There was nothing for it but to wait.

And after five minutes of silence the barrel of a Bereta poked through the door and Steed hit it with a spanner.

"These are very old flats," Steed complained. "Historic, one might almost say, dating back to the early eighteenth century. So I do wish you'd be careful about shooting bullets into the foundations."

The intruder clutched his injured wrist and said nothing. He was a small, sharply dressed fellow who probably always looked as frightened and guilty as he looked now.

"I take it you came here to kill me," said Steed. No answer. "I also assume that you are not a professional, because you went about it very badly." Still nothing. "Who are you?"

The man had a cockney accent when he spoke. "Why didn't you send for the cops?"

"It didn't occur to me."

Steed was still holding the spanner towards the man and he prodded him along the wall until he was underneath the reins, horse brasses and an ancient halter. Steed tipped the halter off the wall and onto the man's shoulders. A quick flip and it was safely round his arms. The man struggled, but he couldn't release himself.

From his pockets Steed discovered that the man was called Alf Knight and he lived in Camden Town. There was no money in his wallet, but he was a member of the Mississippi Club, which probably accounted for the fact.

"We'll dispense with your apologies," said Steed. "Just tell me why you came here."

"I didn't want to kill you, guv. I don't even know who you are. But I was in a jam, you see, and they said . . ."

"They?"

"I owed them a hundred and fifty quid . . ."

He had owed the Mississippi a hundred and fifty pounds, although why any sane man would give Alf Knight so much credit was beyond Steed's understanding. Anyway, Alf had been done over by Mike O'Hara, and then last night Curt Krystal had made him a suggestion.

"They promised me another hundred, as well as writing off the debt . . ."

Alf had a wife and two kids to support, so what would you have done, I ask you? And he was a compulsive gambler, so I mean. "A man's got to live, hasn't he? I didn't mean you no harm, did I, not personally."

Steed took the poor fool upstairs, gave him a few crusts of bread and a cup of coffee. A little homily on dabbling in crime without the right qualifications, and then Steed gave him a hundred and fifty pounds of the government's money. "From now on you owe Krystal nothing, and you do as I say. If you let me down I'll cut off your hands."

"You're a proper gentleman, guv," said Alf. "I won't let you down."

"I expect you will. What were you sent to prison for?"

"What, me? Well, I was framed by the cops. No, I didn't do it, honest I didn't. Well, they said it was burglary. Yes, I suppose it was me as did the job, but they didn't catch me. They just thought I done it. At least, the evidence was fixed. I'm a bleedin' good burglar. Normally. I didn't expect you to have this place wired up with fancy gadgets. Yes, I'm sorry. How was I to know you were listening to some records? Yes, I'm sorry. You just tell me what you want me to do. . . ."

7

"I thought you didn't like places like this," Emma said with a superior smile.

"I don't. We've come here for your benefit." These laboratories always made Steed suspect that science was for retarded schoolboys, men who have never grown out of the stinks and spells phase. But Emma seemed eager for the tour. She smiled at him as they passed through a room of Rhesus monkeys in various stages of disease to show that she had partly forgiven Steed for his rudeness.

The tension between them had flared briefly when they met at the airport. Emma was dressed in a purple velvet trouser dress, which was strikingly suitable for the dismal weather, but Steed had been taken aback by the white kid helmet. "Shouldn't that be made of chain mail?" he had asked. Her nose and eyes were visible through a vizor of perspex. But as she said, "I have come back via Paris."

"You look," Steed had said, "as if you've come back from the crusades."

"Here we are," said Steed as they reached the room where the rats made their contribution to human knowledge. The room was lined with cages up to the ceiling, and each cage contained one large grey rat. "This is Dr. James, who does the experiments."

"Ah, delighted. Mrs. Peel." The white coated doctor looked up from the tiny operating table. He winked at them both in turn and twitched his right shoulder. "I won't be a moment with this subject."

Steed had never felt sympathy for rats before, but the hundreds of sad, button eyes staring at him seemed to ask it. He murmured something about sacrifices on the altar of a new religion, and Dr. James glared at him.

"We do have a licence from the Ministry, Mr. Steed."

"I thought of going into the ministry once," said Steed. "But my certainties faded." He watched the doctor insert several tiny wires into the brain of the anaesthetised rat. This sort of thing was all right for progressive young ladies with degrees in zoology at Bahia University, but Steed was squeamish.

The progressive young lady was asking brightly pertinent questions about the terminals screwed likes mitres in to the skulls of the rats.

"We can fix electrodes in the brain without these leads to the control panel," said Dr. James. "We can control them by radio, but for our purposes this is simpler."

Once the new rat had been wired up he was placed in a glass case and put through his scientific paces. A small stimulus in one part of its brain had the exhilarated animal leaping about in joy; another stimulus reduced the rat to absolute lethargy, and stimulation in a third area sent it ravenously after food. Emma was vastly impressed, and she held forth for a moment on the application of these discoveries to mental illness.

"Or mental non-conformity," Steed intruded cryptically.

"Don't be reactionary," Emma said briskly. "I've seen plenty of catatonics in mental institutions. Brilliant people who've suddenly cracked up. And nothing could be done for them!"

"I thought people like that were electrocuted," said Steed. "Although in pre-history one American tribe bashed their psychopaths on the foreheads with a pointed rock. Those who survived weren't cured but they were more socially amenable. It was a way of keeping down trouble-makers." Steed smiled proudly at his erudition, but he noticed a dangerous flush coming into Emma's cheeks. "They call it a pre-frontal lobotomy," he continued hastily.

"Quite. You make it sound like a nature cure."

"Dr. James's work is perfectly capable of being misused. That's why I've brought you here this morning. Sit down and watch the rat pounding that bar with its foot. You'll soon have a doubt or so yourself."

Emma took a deep breath, removed her helmet in

submission, and then sighed. "All right, Steed, tell me what this is all about."

"It's about power over men's minds," Steed announced, with a diffident shrug at his own sensationalism. "Dr. James is going to give us a lecture."

Steed had last seen rats like those, controlled by electrodes and learning such games as finding their way through a maze, when he had paid a return visit to the Victorian home of Madame Petrova. He had waited until twelve o'clock and then gone off to Putney for a spot of burgling with Alf Knight.

"I don't like it, guv. I've never burgled nowhere with a cop beside me. I mean, it don't seem right somehow. Driving to a job in this bloody great car. It's almost like it was legal."

Steed had assured the man that they would be in real trouble if they were caught, and that was some consolation. Thorburn had reported that Tamara was at the Mississippi, but the Chinese girls were likely to be at home. "And by the way, don't call me a cop. I'm sensitive about things like that."

Alf had quietened down when they reached the house and he became absorbed in his professional task. He took three minute to open the kitchen window, then he clambered in and opened the back door to Steed.

"It's all fitted out with burglar alarms," he whispered, "but nothing like your place. We just have to be quiet."

Steed acknowledged the compliment and went into the house. He flicked out his pencil torch. There was nothing on the ground floor to interest him, ex-

cept the bell push which Tamara had pressed to
summon her bodyguard. The wires went down into
the floorboards, and presumably through into the
basement. But before he left the lounge Steed slipped
the tape from the tape recorder into his pocket. And
he made Alf put back the silver cigarette box.

The door to the cellar was under the stairs, and it
opened easily in response to Alf's hairpin. The old
house creaked mysteriously from time to time and
occasionally Steed could hear the rustling of draughts
between the stays. The cellar contained a quantity
of Victorian junk, nothing more.

"Tap the walls," Steed instructed.

Alf Knight tapped the walls while Steed prodded
the floor with the tip of his umbrella. At last Alf
found a hollow section of the wall, and ten minutes
later they discovered where to open it. "They always
have a hinge somewhere," Alf hissed, "and when
you've found the hinge you're found where to force
it open. Opposite."

The concealed door swung open and a blaze of
light switched on. Steed waited for the reaction, but
nothing happened, so they went into the room, in
silence.

"Gor Christ," said Alf, "a bleedin' zoo. Don't they
smell?"

The cages filled with rats, the operating table, the
instrument panels and the wires. It was a fully
equipped laboratory, if anything more up to date than
the London University research establishment, and
the equipment was Russian. It was a tribute to the
universality of knowledge that the experiments

were much the same, with the extra touch that one of the subjects was a man.

The man was in a torpor, and he only mumbled when Steed tried to shake him into a response. His bed was a pile of straw in the corner of the room, and he was obviously so far from normal life that he wasn't even tied up. He was unshaven, unwashed, and waiting for death.

"What are they doing with the poor bastard?" asked Alf.

"I don't know." Steed had heard only vaguely about these steps forward in brain surgery, but the terminals on the skulls of the rats made it pretty obvious. He examined the man's head, which had a bandage round the temples. The only way to be certain was to fiddle with the instruments panel until the man sprang into ecstatic life.

Steed became absorbed in the dials and switches, and the slight movement behind him didn't register until Alf Knight screamed. Then Alf's body crashed heavily against the wall.

"Don't move, Mr. Steed. This gun is loaded."

The three Chinese bodyguards were ranged in front of the door, and one of them held a gun. The other two moved slowly into the room prepared to toss Steed about the place as they had tossed Alf Knight.

"Isn't this rather taking advantage of a gentleman?" Steed asked amiably. "I mean, what does a chap do when he's faced with three girls in those pyjama things?" He had a rough idea, and he backed away to the side of the room. Alf groaned and sat up with a great effort. "You can't get away with this, you know, not for long."

It was true. Tamara's efforts at espionage were so crude that Steed was seriously worried. There was obviously a lot more involved than a few secrets from a few top civil servants. After all, the woman was even thinking of writing her memoirs, and where would she be by that time? In Holloway, or back in Russia, perhaps.

One of the Chinese girls twisted Alf's arm up behind his head and sprang him to his feet with another scream. The other was smiling as she followed Steed round the edge of the cages.

"We don't have to get away with it for long, Mr. Steed."

"Don't talk," snapped the girl with the gun. "Chop him."

There was no alternative, and British standards of fair play took a sudden dive. Steed brushed his upheld hands against the cage doors of two alert-looking rats, and then as the doors swung open he moved apologetically aside and opened two more doors. It was a few seconds before the girls realised what was happening, and then as a flurry of brown fur scuttled across the floor their inscrutable faces registered panic.

With a muttered thanksgiving that the girls were also feminine—and afraid of rats—Steed swept the rest of the cages to the ground. The rats squealed and the girls were screaming in a general rush towards the door. Steed smashed up some of the equipment to add to the confusion, and then hauled Alf Knight to his feet.

"Are you fit?" he demanded.

Alf mumbled that he was.

"All right, pick up that man and follow me!"

They ran to the foot of the cellar stairs where Steed retrieved his umbrella. He tripped up the first girl with the handle of his brolly, pushed the three of them together and back down the stairs. While they squirmed about on the floor with several rats, Steed led the way to the ground floor.

"Come on, man, he can't weigh more than seven stone!"

"Sorry, guv."

Steed pulled them into the hallway and then locked the cellar door behind them. It would be a while before the noise down there subsided. He adjusted his tie, glanced at the angle of his bowler in the hall mirror, and led the way down the garden path.

"We shall never know who he is, I'm afraid, Mr. Steed. He has a mental age of eighteen months. He gurgles a little, and now he smiles at one of the female nurses, but we've had to bottle-feed him. He just doesn't respond at all."

Steed was becoming haunted by men in white coats and the surgical spirit smell of these places. The doctor was earnest, well meaning, and yet remote from his patients. Justifiably. The man on the bed was disturbing. They'd shaved him, to make him look nice for the visitor, and they'd put a clean nappy on him, but Steed felt sick at the sight. He never had liked mental hospitals, of course, the male nurses frightened him. During a brief period of sensitivity some years ago he had dreamed that he was in an asylum and all the reasonable doctors were saying, yes, Mr. Steed, of course you can go home, as soon as you convince us that you are sane . . . just prove it. Years ago.

"Do you think," Steed asked the doctor, "that places like this are society's revenge on people it doesn't understand?"

"I beg your pardon?"

"What have they done to this man?"

"They've given him a drug known as sodium amytol, which is useful when you're dealing with paranoid schizophrenia. We have to break down the defence mechanisms, you see, and avoid all the normal thought processes and attitudes that have been built up over many years. The easiest way to do this is either to obliterate them, which is done by a sizeable electric shock, or to take the patient back to babyhood and then let him, as it were, grow up again mentally. Quite often a patient develops more naturally the second time, and mental quirks that were produced by a specific social environment don't recur."

"So what," Steed asked, looking at the man on the bed, "has gone wrong?"

"Lack of proper supervision, I should think. This often used to happen, ten years ago, but now we understand the drug better."

The man on the bed began to cry, and the doctor

watched frowning for a moment. "Shall we go into my office? It will be quieter in there."

"I didn't come here for quiet," said Steed. "I want to talk to him, to this man."

"No can do, I'm afraid—"

"Of course you can," Steed urged. "The fellow has electrodes in his brain. Wire him up, that's all you need to do, and he'll be like a puppet for as long as the current lasts."

The doctor bit his lip. "I wonder if you're right."

"Well you should know. Science and all that stuff; I'd have thought you wired people up like that all the time."

He seemed a little pained at Steed's unsympathetic attitude to medicine. But he summoned two burly male nurses and told them to take the patient into radiography.

Steed followed, muttering to himself about the medical research they did at Auschwitz, and the almost healthy attitude of the past when people had simply laughed at lunatics. He chain-smoked four panatellas while they fiddled with wires, currents and strength-impulses. The patient screamed, twitched, fell unconscious, became hysterical, reacted in various ways that demonstrated the range of human behaviour and probably enlarged the frontiers of human knowledge.

After half an hour the man told them that his name was Hank Robinson. Success. He turned out to be an American. But during the half hour or so that the institution could afford to keep this equipment running he was far more concerned with his own problems. He kept asking questions, such as where he was and what had happened, what were they going to do with him?

"We're trying to help you," said Steed. "Some very ruthless people have been hurting you, and I want to stop them."

"What are these pains in my head? Because, Christ, these aren't just headaches. I keep getting these damned explosions."

Steed carried on talking to him, quietly, reasonably, trying not to make any promises because Hank Robinson's only way out would be a quick and easy death. Eventually he pieced together a picture of what had happened.

Hank Robinson was an ambitious American who had come to England when the gambling clubs had become legal. And the Mafia had got him. He had owned a joint on the south coast, expanded, established a chain of small houses and then tried to open up in London. That had been his last mistake.

"I was dragged off to some place near Brighton, where they tortured me and did all weird things, I don't remember what. There were about ten people there, and we all got beaten up and given drugs, funny stuff, by these Chinese girls. . . . It was like a factory, only I don't remember much. I think I was taken away from there. To somewhere else. They cut me up, did operations. . . ."

He began crying again. He was scared of all these people, and within five minutes he was asking for his mother. She would look after him. He trembled, wet his bed, and then became a baby. Maybe he was better off that way.

Steed went home feeling disturbed and indignant. Tamara's casual contempt for human life was so awe-inspiring. It was difficult to understand and impossible to remedy. Her attitude was of terrible self-indulgence, as if she were pulling the wings off butterflies.

8

Emma Peel worked as a croupier for several nights before anything happened to convince her that the Mississippi was connected with Tamara Petrova's activities. The club was scarcely law-abiding, of course, and Curt Krystal was a villain, but she could not see it as a hive of espionage. Russian agents, surely, would choose a more discreet 'front' than a corner of London's gang-land!

But Emma went loyally to work at 7.30 every evening and returned home at 4.15 every morning. She had fitted herself out with cowgirl gear, and now her only problem was whether supper was breakfast or lunch was afternoon tea, her only worry was what nightwork might do to her complexion, and she lost any fascination she might have had about the role of chance in a man's life.

The house won, every night, and Emma could see with utter certainty that some men were doomed and some women merely hooked, and no one who came for the excitement of losing could expect to win. Curt Krystal didn't need to load the dice or stack the cards, because gamblers always lose, and on the occasions when they win they lose their winnings as well.

So much for the myth established by cowboy films.

The only possible explanation was that gamblers *wanted* to lose. Emma knew that with a little intelligent study they could sometimes win, and they *could* stop when the game was running in their favour, they could even go home when they had lost as much as they could afford. But no; they lost. The sensible gamblers stayed, presumably, in the bingo halls and the whist drives. Only suicidal masochists played the big games—millionaires who felt guilty of their riches, business men who resented their money and playboys who craved humiliation. Something like that.

Emma had known men who enjoyed hunting dangerous animals, she had braved the rough seas in small boats with her father at the age of eleven, and she had understood her husband, whose wildness had eventually killed him. All men gamble with something.

Perhaps it was the women who drove men on, she thought, those women who send their men off to war, and who adore a reckless gambler, until he loses. There seemed to be a sexual excitement in the game for these women; Emma could see their flush and physical heat, as if this were a wrestling match and the men were trying to impress them. But such women's contempt for the loser was so total that their whole resentment of the male sex was probably involved.

The same attitude explained why Curt Krystal enjoyed his work. He loved to watch men being ruined, or men afraid. Emma found him horribly fascinating. He perspired and his breathing quickened when he watched ten thousand pounds placed on a card. He was a sadist relishing the gambler's fear. And the crowd that invariably gathered round a big-time loser always found his defeat funny. But it was only funny, Emma felt, to people who laugh when a man slips on a banana skin and kills himself.

"Yes, well dear," said Cynthia, "I always say that sex is behind everything, don't you?"

Emma smiled stoically. "Not often."

But sex did seem to be basic in this business, and Emma found it bewildering. The most popular legend of the casino was its Shylock Stakes, which a few people had seen played and everybody talked about in hushed tones. It was the obsession of the pathological gambler, the ultimate stake that a man can risk. When a man has lost everything he can then chance his pound of flesh.

"Oh well, we all despise the customers, dear." Cynthia was a chirpy cowgirl who had taken Emma under her protection. "I just make sure that when they're throwing their money away a bit of it comes in my direction."

Emma tried to sound broad minded. She said that she found a horrible fascination in watching a man systematically ruining himself, and that worried her. It had become a spectator sport, as if Skid Row had become a tourist attraction.

"You're the sort of girl," Cynthia said with a shrug, "who doesn't watch road accidents."

"I don't." Emma wondered whether she lacked experience of real life.

Cynthia was a small girl with red hair and a body like a seaside postcard, all curves and bottom, bulges and cheerful vulgarity. It was said that she collected more coats at the cloakroom than Waterloo Station; men brought coats at the height of summer to leave them with Cynthia, and defeated men were rumoured to ask for coats they had never possessed, to be reassured that they had come in "just as you are, dearie." An illegitimate daughter at a convent boarding school was supposed to complete the old, old picture of the golden hearted tart.

"Did you see who came in tonight?" Cynthia asked as they were changing out of their wild west working clothes. "Poor old Alf Knight. I reckon they'll kill him."

Alf Knight? Emma tried to remember what Steed had said about him. "What did he come in for?"

"They brought him in." Cynthia struggled to squeeze her flesh into a green plastic sheath. "I heard Mr. Krystal saying that he would nail Alf's feet to the floor. Poor old Alf. Just because he owes a couple of hundred."

Emma Peel said good morning to Cynthia on the gang plank and went back to fetch her spurs. "I want to have the points filed down," she explained. "I drew blood this evening, from a German industrialist who kept calling me Pocohontas." She went aboard behind three small women who were chattering to each other in Chinese.

"Mrs. Peel," Curt Krystal drawled behind her, "what do you want?" He moved silently for a big man. "Go home."

"I was going to—"

"Go home."

There was something unarguable in Krystal's expression, to do with those translucent eyes buried in folds of unhealthy flesh. Emma smiled radiantly and left. She went back onto the embankment and walked along to a rowing boat that was easily stolen. It was a mild evening, but too icy in the water for a January swim. Emma rowed back to the Mississippi and stopped by the port hole of Curt Krystal's office.

She waited for several minutes, steadying the boat and accustoming herself to the rhythmic lapping of waves, adjusting her ears to the muffled voices, and then she leaned up to glance quickly through the glass.

Alf Knight was strapped in a chair in the middle of the office. He was stark naked and screaming with pain at the interrogation methods of the Chinese girls. Emma Peel could just see Curt Krystal on the far side, lounging with one of his henchmen and listening to the yells. The gang boss didn't seem unduly worried about Alf's double-cross.

"All we want to know," he drawled casually, "is who this guy Steed is working for, and why he's poking around."

"I don't know, guv—" He broke off with a shriek as one of the girls pressed a spot in his neck. "He said something about government money—that's all I know."

"Think."

To help him think a Chinese girl put a lighted cigarette to his navel. That caused a lot of noise and it amused Mr. Krystal, but it didn't help Alf to remember what he didn't know. By the time the cigarette had burned itself down Alf was pleading and crying in a totally undignified manner and his body was spattered with raging blisters. When the girl changed to lighted matches and set fire to the crinkly tuft of hair below Alf's armpit he begged them to kill him.

Emma listened to these proceedings with impotent feelings of nausea. She wondered what possible pleasure they could get from torturing a repulsive middle aged man. Even a sadist would need to be perverted to enjoy inflicting pain on scraggy Alf Knight. But Krystal seemed to find it gratifying, and the Chinese girls seemed to work with relish. It took about twenty minutes for them to grow bored.

"Your job was to kill this man Steed, wasn't it?"

"I know, sir, but now that I've paid you the money. . . ."

"Kill him, as soon as you find out his game."

"All right, guv." Emma could feel the wretched man tugging his forelock.

"Keep in with him, and work with him. Only this time report to me every morning. Okay?"

"You see, guv, it was like this. . . ."

Emma let the boat drift a hundred yards downstream and then went off to Westminster. She felt rather pleased to be getting Steed out of bed at five in the morning. He would realise what unholy hours she was keeping to preserve his beloved country.

As she walked down Westminster Mews she had a strange sensation of being watched, and a shadow passed the end of the passage as she rang Steed's bell. But it must have been her fancy. Nobody was around at this hour of night. Steed came to the door looking disappointingly urbane in his blue velvet dressing gown, as if he had been waiting all night for just this pleasure.

"I'm afraid it would be irresponsible of me to offer you a brandy, Mrs. Peel, in spite of your dissolute way of life. Perhaps a tomato juice would appeal to you? You look disturbed."

Emma told him about the unspeakable way Alf Knight had been treated by the slug-like Krystal. She was still wrought up and angry with herself for not being able to help.

"Poor Alf was born unlucky," Steed said airily,

and then he began to discuss his own safety. There were times when Steed annoyed her.

"Can I offer you a plate of cornflakes?" he asked, as he saw perceptively that he had annoyed her.

"No. Just look after yourself." Sometimes he didn't deserve the massive concern that people lavished on him. He had probably been spoiled even as a child. And to think that occasionally Emma felt positively fond of the man!

"I'm moving out of London for about three weeks," he said to reassure her. "Going up north to fight an election. That should be safe enough."

"But you can't. . . ."

Steed yawned, just to show that he was human. "I've been warned off. It seems that M.I.5 have taken exception to the way I've been blundering about and now that I've stirred things up a bit I'm being moved so that you can look after the situation."

"I haven't the foggiest idea what it's all about."

"Just as well. Poor old Cyril Maxton seems to have known, and he was run over. He'd been in touch with security that afternoon because he wanted to tell someone why Smeck-Hudson committed suicide. The whole affair has got M.I.5 rushing all over the place in utter confusion."

She watched Steed go over to the tape recorder and fiddle with the knobs. Then she listened to the tape, which consisted of squeals and laughter and a few heavy thuds. It was all rather kinky.

"This," said Steed, "is partly why Smeck-Hudson committed suicide. He was beaten up by the three

Chinese girls and then thrown out. Tamara with typical female love of mementoes has taped the whole session."

There was the predictable melodramatic stuff about how Smeck-Hudson made her sick when he touched her, how she had made these sacrifices for her country, and an embarrassing bit where he pleaded. Then more yelling and hilarity as the Chinese girls threw him out of the window.

"Never trust a beautiful Russian spy," said Steed at the end of it, "because underneath it all they're just like any other woman—bloody dangerous."

Emma shuddered. "I don't see the sense of sending you to Brawhill. It will waste too much time."

"Never mind," Steed laughed. "I have faith in you, Mrs. Peel. I'm sure that by the time I'm elected to parliament you'll have the whole thing wrapped up."

Emma found that she was drowsily nodding off, on the sofa. Even when he was being most insular she couldn't help feeling secure in Steed's presence. She would be sleeping like a baby within ten minutes, and then what would the daily woman say? She asked him whether the record had come through from America about Krystal.

"Oh yes, didn't I tell you? He seems to be a top man in the Mafia. That would account for the Sicilian who appointed you to the job. Krystal worked his way up through the casinos of Las Vegas, and he became so big that they've created this empire for him to avoid an internal war. He was given the British Empire, so to speak." Steed chuckled irritatingly at his own joke.

"How does the Mafia tie in with Russia?"

"Goodness knows," said Steed unconcernedly. "I expect you to tell me when I come back to London."

9

Steed was certain that Alf Knight would never try to kill him; Alf had the sergeant major mentality and he was becoming quite devoted to Major John Steed (retd.). Curt Krystal had given him two instructions, to kill and to report, perhaps to ensure that Alf carried out the lesser instruction. Alf reported every day from Brawhill in letters of monolithic illiteracy.

"Mr. S spends all his time bashing on doors and saying I am your parliamentary candidate and the birds all say oh yes well I dont know about my old man and I will vote for you and the old man says sod off. It gets boring. One bird tried the old come on stuff and Mr S said we didnt have the time but thanks for the kind thought. Most of its what about the blacks and bring back the cat and Mr S says what about the whites and they all start shouting.

In the evenings he spouts in town halls and they all laugh and last night we nearly had a punch up. I'll be glad to get back to London."

Steed only read the first report and after that he relied on Alf's discretion. He had other problems on his mind, such as his agent's assumption that Steed would bring the whole construction of party politics crashing to the ground. "There are definite rules to this game, old man," Mr. Wilson repeated three times in the first two days.

The agent had obtained a list from somewhere of all the people in the constituency who would vote for Steed, another list of all those who wouldn't, and a third list of floating voters. In practice the lists were invariably wrong and this meant he wasted time discussing politics instead of paying three hundred courtesy calls a day.

"And I don't see why we have to trail the streets with this character always in tow," said Wilson for the third time. "Is he a bodyguard or something?"

Steed turned to examine Alf's appearance; he looked a little out of place, perhaps, and the vivid rosette made him quite conspicuous. The legend, Take Heed with Steed, was out of character for Alf Knight. But at least he was an obvious supporter.

"Maybe we should have twelve of them," Steed suggested. "It would be more traditional."

That night Alf, who was sensitive, disappeared.

The meetings hall of Brawhill Secondary Modern School was the same as all the other halls, and the audience was the same as well. A sprinkling of party enthusiasts, a group of comedians who had come to heckle and a hundred lethargic nondescripts who must have come in for the warm. The usual bawling baby. Local party eminences on the platform beside him who harped on about his war record. . . . And that hatchet faced man who always sat at the back and did the *Daily Telegraph* crossword puzzle; he had been following Steed for days.

"What this country needs is men with courage and independence, originality and a fresh approach," said Councillor Waite, who had sacked men for less, "politicians who will combine the best of the past with the forces of the future, to produce a Britain with vigour, dynamism and abrasiveness. Here is such a man—Major John Steed."

A smattering of polite applause as Steed adjusted his buttonhole and walked round to the side of the table. He wondered how children who spent their lives in this dreary school could possibly develop a vision of the perfect society. Sylvia loves Eric was carved on the table and below that someone had recorded a four letter word, and a little to the left, knickers.

He wondered for the twentieth time what would interest them. "The answer to seven across," he announced solemnly, "*Mrs. Leo Hunter,* is lioness. I did that crossword in bed this morning when I should have been visiting the local prison." The man in the back row glanced up impassively, then wrote in the word lioness.

"I couldn't face the prospect of going to that prison, and if I were a prisoner there I'd try to escape. The place is a disgrace. I'm surprised you have anybody prepared to go there. . . ." It was an effective way of introducing his speech on crime and the penal reform set out in the party manifesto, and it provoked the hecklers to shout the obvious remarks, they aren't supposed to want to go there—it's a deterrent and so forth.

"Newgate prison was also a deterrent," said Steed, "but it was so barbaric that they pulled it down and built a post office. That was a hundred years ago. I'm surprised that we're still arguing about that issue."

He was developing a taste for the appreciative laughter that some of his cracks produced, and he wondered whether political life wasn't bad for the character. Yesterday the audience had been heckling about hanging as a deterrent and the danger of hanging the wrong man; Steed said that hanging the wrong man was probably an even greater deterrent than hanging the right one, especially if it was done in public, and the meeting had been in uproar for ten minutes. Mr. Wilson expected to be bald by polling day.

"What about arming the police?" someone called out.

"If the army's standard of marksmanship is anything to go by," said Steed, "they'd miss every time and the streets would be a constant hazard of stray bullets."

One of the games that Steed played with himself was to try to provoke a response from the hatchet face at the back, but he never had smiled, and now as Steed launched into the final peroration on making Britain safe for old ladies and the under-privileged alike he knew that he wouldn't draw a tear from the man. "Vote for me and I'll take the vengeance out of justice. Every vote for me is a step towards ending pointless fights between differently dressed adolescents and towards making our homes safe from interference."

The subject for the evening was crime. When he got back to his hotel Alf Knight was watching television, and he was dressed in a ghastly brown check suit that Steed had never seen before.

"I've been here all evening, guv—"

"Nonsense, you've been working!"

In Alf's room there was a suitcase, heavy with a portable typewriter, table lighter, some deplorable brass ornaments and odd pieces of jewellery. But it was a first edition of a book, *The Economic Consequences of Mr. Churchill* that gave him away. "To my friend Horace Wilson," signed, "John Maynard Keynes."

Alf had taken his revenge on the party agent.

Steed rang down for a bottle of brandy, lit a panatella, and instructed Alf to follow him into his own room. "If you will steal yourself a new suit," he said wearily, "you should steal one that is more discreet. That hideous, vulgar pattern makes you look like an unsuccessful bookmaker." He then went through the motions of telling Alf about the advantages of honesty, because Alf would expect it.

"Well he riled me this morning, you see. I meant to go straight, you see—"

"The main reason you should go straight is that you're so damned inefficient. Hold your head up, man, and look honest!" The sudden military tone startled Alf, but he couldn't look honest. He fidgeted his feet and glanced furtively at Steed out of the corner of his eyes. "No wonder you've spent nearly ten years altogether in gaol. How much money have you earned from crime?"

Alf scratched his head. "About—I don't know. A few hundred quid."

"You'd have made more money from sweeping roads. No wonder people such as Curt Krystal despise you. He makes several hundred thousand pounds a year. He's a business man, that's why the Mafia is so powerful. There's no place in crime any more for the small man who goes off and burgles a flat on his own behalf. All that became as dated as the small family grocer when the Great Train Robbery showed what supermarket methods could achieve."

"Yea, you're quite right, Mr. Steed. I'll break in tomorrow and put it all back, and then honest to God I'll go straight. I won't do it again."

Steed sent him off to bed and then relaxed with a large brandy. You couldn't expect a good Napoleon in Brawhill, but a Remy Martin goes down well after a day of political nonsense. Steed looked across the city square to the town hall, the theatre and the Victorian office blocks. They were all the same, these provincial cities, they must have been built in the same year by the same architect. How odd that they should be so comfortable, and in a way so earnest, like the Bishopsgate area of London. A shame that the snow had all melted away beneath the trams and the heavy traffic.

He had been worried about something, but now he couldn't remember what it was. Oh yes, the hatchet face with the *Daily Telegraph*. Steed was sure that he worked for M.I.5, you could always tell by the air of being an Englishman abroad; even in London they looked like an Englishman abroad. And Steed wanted to know why M.I.5 had objected to him so strongly that he had been sent up here out of the way.

Tomorrow he would have a chat with the fellow.

Steed finished his nightcap and then undressed for bed, cleaned his teeth and drew back the curtains. It was all a ritual. As he turned out the light he bent over the shade and said, "This is your friendly station signing off for the night. Normal broadcasting will be resumed at eight thirty tomorrow morning. I do hope you won't have grown bored by polling day, because every vote counts. Thank you and good night."

He slept soundly, woke refreshed, and at breakfast sat at the same table as the hatchet faced man.

"Good morning."

The man grunted.

"Looks like another splendid day for making snow men. If you enjoy that kind of exercise. Have you read Peter Simple yet?"

"No."

"No. You don't look like a man who laughs before

breakfast." Steed picked elegantly at his sunshine cereal. "Do you find this city exciting?"

"I don't know what you mean."

"Exciting? Was once referring to perhaps as a stimulant. Seven letters."

The man glared, folded up his newspaper and pushed away his cup of tea. "I can't make out whether you're a fool, Mr. Steed, or a dangerous lunatic. But whichever you are I find it a strain on my nerves."

"You should change your job. I know a couple of fellows in M.I.5 and they've been getting steadily more neurotic for years."

"What are you talking about?"

"Military Intelligence, isn't that your line? No no, I'm not being sarcastic. You've been following me around for days looking like Valentine Dyall, bugging my bedroom and generally behaving in a most unfriendly way. Quite noticeable. So I went through the list of possibilities: a Russian spy—no, because you're too thin; too unfriendly to be an American, not seedy enough to be a private detective; you have to be M.I.5."

The man's face had gone pallid with rage. "I'm a reporter!" He slapped his paper under his arm and strode from the dining room, leaving Steed chuckling happily at the droll humour of the man in black.

But within an hour Steed was back on the streets, shaking hands with the inheritors of woman's suffrage, assuring an angry nightworker that he hadn't come round to knock it off with that bitch of a wife, "delightful though the lady appears," and listening sympathetically to Wilson's account of the burglary. The days were long in Brawhill.

10

"Mrs. Peel," he said softly, "I'd like to know where you went the night before last. After you left here."

"I assume you know. People only ask a question like that when they think they know the answer."

"I'll tell you why, Mrs. Peel." For some reason Emma laughed brightly at her own cleverness and sat on the edge of Krystal's desk. "Surely you haven't been spying on me? I mean, if you aren't satisfied with my work it would be simpler to fire me." Emma smiled sadly. "And I was beginning to enjoy myself here."

"I've been spying on a Mr. Steed. How long have you known him?"

"Since I came to work here. He pestered me for days to go and see him, because he said he was barred from coming into the club. Eventually I gave in and promised to have a word with you."

Krystal picked up a paper knife and prodded Emma's bottom off the edge of his desk. "All right, have a word with me."

She wondered whether it would solve anything to pitch him through the port hole. "Well, he's rich and silly, and determined to be poor and silly. I can't see why you object to him."

Krystal suddenly took a bottle of Scotch and two glasses from his drawer. A non-proprietary brand. And his dough-face split into a sinister smile. "Because he was prying."

Emma accepted the drink. She hadn't expected this suspiciously friendly move. But she told herself not to be so nervous and waited to see what would happen.

"In one sense, Mrs. Peel, I have been watching you, because you have style. I find you very attractive." He walked round behind her and scrutinised Emma's defiant body. "You excite my customers." Another prod with the paper knife. "Yes," he said approvingly, "so unattainable, so English. You are like a thoroughbred racehorse. I should like to work more closely with you."

Why thank you kind sir.

A large pudgy hand settled itself on Emma's thigh in a squeeze of friendship. She removed it. "I don't think you appreciate the kind of man I am, Mrs. Peel. I am civilised, I have been cultivating your B.B.C. accent—"

I didn't mean to laugh.

"But I'm an immigrant at heart. My family came from Sicily when Sicily wasn't a fashionable place to come from. My father worked on the waterfront for thirty dollars a week and a lot of weeks he didn't have the good fortune to work. The years before the war were tough on my seven brothers and six sisters. We went to school and learned our lessons in the streets of Brooklyn, and then when we were twelve we went to work where the money was. You know what I mean? I just want you to understand me, if you're going to be working more closely with me. Otherwise you might be shocked some day. . . ."

I've seen the films—Edward G. Robinson. Nobody messes with Little Caesar. Because now I'm on Easy Street, baby. A finger thoughtfully along the upper lip. A coin flipped and caught and flipped endlessly. I'm tough, baby!

"I know, Curt, you're someone," Emma said sweetly. "Just remember that I'm someone as well. I'm Emma Peel." She took the sweating palm from her waist and went to the door. "I'm sure we'll work very well together."

She opened the door with a sharp jerk and thrust out her foot as the man stumbled in to meet her blow to the carotid artery. She was showing off, perhaps, but it worked. "Don't shoot!" she heard Krystal snap as she went back to the roulette wheel.

The only problem was that Krystal would be just as close to Emma as she was to him. It was obviously part of his scheme, because he had his doubts. Emma decided that she herself wouldn't have believed that story about Steed pestering her. But then she knew Steed; he made sure people pestered

him. Thank God she had established her indiffer-
ence to Krystal's thugs.

At half past four she walked down the gang plank
and found one of those Kandy Koloured Tangerine things waiting for her. "Get in," said Krystal.
"I'll give you a lift home."

She climbed in the car beside him, but they
didn't move. Krystal was staring at the silhouette
of his boat against the neon signs across the water
and listening to its sounds in the night. "Do you
know where," he asked eventually, "I had the idea
for my Mississippi river boat?"

"From reading Damon Runyon?"

"I thought of it when I was visiting your Oxford. They have similar barges moored on the
Thames, just rotting, used by the students for
changing rooms. I believe they were left there by
the livery companies of London. Such a shame to
neglect them like that." He tore his eyes from the
monument to his own power; the pause for reflec-
tion was over. "Oakhill Park, Hampstead," he com-
manded.

The chauffeur's head perched squarely on his
shoulders with no fancy neck to break up the line,
and his ears jutted out to keep up the peaked cap.
Emma always found the back view of chauffeurs
slightly comic. She wondered how he manoeuvred
this fantastic car when there was traffic on the roads.
"An ideal car for large families," Emma com-
mented.

"American standards are different now," Krystal

said heavily, "from what they were before the War of Independence."

"So I believe."

They swept through the streets in silence for several minutes, startled once by a few bars of 'By Yon Bonnie Braes' on the hooter when a dog wandered in front of the car and a second time when they swung into Frognal at forty-five miles an hour and Emma thought she would be tipped out. When they skidded to a halt outside the block of luxury flats Krystal spoke again.

"I presume you've heard of these Pan-American gambling parties? About fifteen very rich gamblers hire a jet and come to England for the weekend; a few hundred thousand dollars change hands and then they go back on Monday."

"We all have our vices," said Emma.

"They like everything just right. Have you been in my private gaming rooms?"

"No."

"I want you to be banker on Saturday. The game will probably last for two days, but it will be worth our while. All right?" His smile was like the hangman's at eight o'clock and he put out his hand. Normally they twist your arm and blindfold you when you respond. "We should see some fun."

She breathed in quickly and he just missed her nipples. "I'm looking forward to it." She jumped out of the car, waved as if it had been a perfectly marvellous evening, and went up to her penthouse on the top floor. Eight storeys up. It was on the roof really.

She closed the front door and leant against it, breathing heavily. There was something splendidly remote up here, on the roof of London, and sometimes when she stood looking out of the massive wall of glass that was the southern side she understood the exhilaration her husband had felt, that made it necessary for him to fly higher and higher, faster and faster, until it killed him. And when she got like that she felt a gnawing sense of anguish in the pit of her stomach, almost a pain that was empty and defeated—yet it was pleasant because she was with him again, or at least sharing things he had felt and it seemed as if they were close. But he was dead. And she had to prevent herself from crying, because crying was also pleasant, it brought the idea of him closer and she was emotionally involved with him again. After four years, she thought irritably, and still she was liable to all this stuff at five o'clock in the morning. She rang up Steed.

"Hello," she said brightly, "I thought I ought to let you know the latest developments."

"I was just dreaming about you," said Steed. "I'm relieved to hear that it was all a nightmare. What are you doing?"

"Oh, getting in with Curt Krystal and things like that. He seems to approve of me, and I'm going to be his special banker for a private orgy. I might even end up as a gangster's moll."

"My dear Mrs. Peel, how clever of you."

"You might sound concerned!"

"If it were anybody less fiendishly capable of keeping gorillas in their place, I should be. As it is,

I feel apprehensive for Mr. Krystal. Tell me about this private orgy."

Emma told him as she was getting undressed.

"I want you to find out exactly who these people are. They must be coming over here for more than a gambling spree."

"Why?"

"Because of the timing. Tamara Petrova has apparently disappeared and three foreign newspapers are serialising her life story. In it she claims to be a spy. There's quite a scandal developing, and it seems to be our job to hush the whole thing up."

"So who," Emma asked, "do you expect these Americans to be? Mafia bosses or something?"

"I don't know." She could hear yawning noises from the other end of the line, and Steed said that she must be tired. "Oh, by the way," he added as she was putting down the phone, "do be careful of yourself."

Emma went to bed feeling distinctly irritated with Steed, which was quite a common condition for her. Who was he to be apprehensive for Krystal? But she fell asleep within half a minute and soon began dreaming that Madame Petrova was seducing Steed. She woke up feeling much more cheerful.

The fifteen jet set gamblers did not look like the inheritors of Al Capone's empire. And most of them were too old to be playboys. They looked more like an international convention of undertakers. They had been playing check pinochle all the way over the Atlantic and their conversation was entirely concerned with analysing the games. They scarcely looked at Emma.

Over tea they analysed the games they were going to have that night. It was all extremely to the point, and any intrusion of subjects such as making money, or thinking about the political situation, would have been in bad taste. They mentioned once that any tax on players instead of on casinos would be an international disaster, but that hardly rated as political awareness.

Two of them had brought their wives, fluffy brainless things who glared at Emma with all the hatred of neglected toys. The older one, Martha, sat in a corner all day playing patience while the other, Billie, went off to get her hair done by Vidal Sassoon and to buy one of those crazy dresses you know with holes in it. God-dammit she'd read about swinging London. The two of them jerked rhythmically to the constant beat of pop music, which they preferred very loud, and they drank a bottle of gin a day, each. Eventually Emma tried to ignore them, before she became obsessed with the place of women in society.

"We're going down to the south coast tonight, Mrs. Peel." Curt Krystal made the announcement on Saturday evening after a sudden telephone call and a hasty conference with the party. "These are simple tourists," Krystal explained, "they have heard about your Prince of Wales and his Royal Pavilion, so naturally they want to look at the joint."

What could be more natural? It was on the journey down in the Kandy Koloured Tangerine thing that Emma had her brainwave. The youngest member of the team was an excitable Latin character with fleshy good looks and his name was Rick; he drank too much, talked too much, and he was married to Billie. Emma decided to break him.

There was no simple way of finding out why the Mafia had set up a Russian defector to work against the British government, and the only thing to do was assume that Steed was right—these were the men who knew, so one of them had to be jolted into some indiscretion.

"You know, Emma," said Krystal as they were speeding through Epsom, "I get the feeling you still haven't taken to me."

"You don't understand English women," said Emma. "We behave differently from girls like Billie. Perhaps you would prefer someone like her. Is America packed out with her type?"

"She's frigid." Krystal stared at the open E-type in front of them and watched the blonde hair blowing in the icy wind. "And when a girl like Billie is frigid she's nothing." He turned to glance at the car behind them, but Martha's face did nothing to improve the temperature.

"There's no such thing as a frigid woman," Emma said teasingly. "Only men who can't awaken them."

Krystal considered this for a while. "Mrs. Peel, you have a way of bringing conversations to a full stop."

She risked opening a new conversation. "I was

reading in one of the newspapers last week that most of London's clubs are now being run on Mafia money."

"I read it. Your English newspapers are too romantic, they've seen too many American movies. Do you know what the Mafia is? It's a syndicate—not a gang. A kind of co-operative system like the British old boy network. Its main use is for politicians to scare hell out of the American public, unless you're a member, and then its main use is to avoid treading on someone else's toes. It's a business concern. It increases efficiency."

That was all. Not a word about the Sicilian origins. And Emma knew that it derived in much the same way as Mussolini's fascist party, as a peasant movement to fight oppression, and like fascism it had rapidly become a terrorist organisation to keep the peasants in their place. It had become a political organisation in Sicily on the extreme right wing. It was only a political organisation in America to the extent that it bought politicians when the need arose, just as it bought justice or work. It supplied in return dope, sex and casinos. By some values of exchange that was better than most political parties. ——

"What impresses an English woman, Emma? If a man is powerful, and on the point of becoming as powerful as governments, and if that doesn't impress her, what do you recommend?"

Emma shivered. "A government usually impresses people who don't give a damn by locking them up or shooting them."

Krystal laughed delightedly, but the joke was his own.

They didn't go into Brighton; instead they turned off the main road seven miles outside the town and went through a small village to Krystal's country seat. It seemed to be completely isolated, and as they drew up outside the front door Emma could see no lights anywhere. The eighteenth century house loomed over them in Gothic darkness.

The hearty Americans exchanged money on the result of the drive down, because Prinny would have wished it, and then trooped inside the house. They seemed impressed to find that the place had three Chinese domestics, although Martha had to be reassured that they weren't from the mainland.

"What do you make of this house, Emma? Genuine, yes? It was advertised in the *New Yorker* and I decided I just had to have it. When in England like they say. Good?"

"Excellent." Emma smiled at the careful way the agent had filled the rooms with expensive old furniture and antique trinkets. It was like a film set. But Curl Krystal swept through the hall like a squire out of Fielding, bawling orders and announcing their presence, so completely at home that Emma wondered whether they would have to go out hunting in the morning.

"Shin Peng, tell the mistress we're here and have her see me in the library in fifteen minutes. Albert, I want you. The rest of you go through with Tsu Ming and have something to eat. And Emma, if you find the iceberg's transistor too much you can always give us a tune on the harpsichord; the music room is over there."

Krystal was proud of his house, and the jet set were overawed as well, because they had seen advertisements in all the American papers to come to England and see earls and barons in establishments like this. Man, this was class. Billie said zowie, look at the sexy suit of armour.

"Who's the mistress of the house?" Emma asked her.

"Honey, should I know?"

"No," said the guy called Al, "you shouldn't."

"Honey, all I want to know is where the bar fits in."

Martha bawled from the lounge that the oasis was found, and the gaming table was in the same room. Life reverted at once to normal. It was seven hours before Emma saw the mistress of the house, and everybody else had seen her by then. Throughout the evening the men left the table in pairs and went to consult with Krystal in the library. It was a wrench for them, but the business was clearly important.

The players divided up into two tables of six, and Emma made sure she was at the table with Rick. The other four were standard types—they had taken to poker at the age of sixteen and it was part of the process of growing up to read Nelson Algren and try to look like Frank Sinatra—you can't shake that off just because you've become rich. They all looked as if they had golden arms and in their case it wasn't heroin. But they weren't helpless addicts either;

they played a tougher game than Emma had encountered before. They knew how to play, and when to bet, when to turn up a card and when to buy a card to complete a flush. They weren't showing off.

Emma Peel was wearing a diamond ring, which she fiddled with nervously, twirling it round her middle finger and pressing it against the cards during the first thirty minutes of play. It was the Braille system of marking a deck, and it took about thirty minutes. But after half an hour every ace had its imprint on the top left hand corner, every king its imprint a centimetre lower down, every queen a centimetre below that, and so on until every denomination could be felt as she dealt the cards.

After two hours Rick had lost fifty thousand pounds and he was watching everybody to discover who was cheating. But he was looking for somebody who was cheating to win, whereas Emma only cheated when she knew he had a winning hand, at other times the game took its natural course. After three hours Rick was passing cheques, and an hour later he was looking for a fight.

Emma asked him whether it wouldn't be more sensible for him to retire.

"Listen, kid, I'm worth half a million," he snapped.

At four o'clock in the morning she was being maternal and suggested he go to bed. "You don't need to impress us," she urged, "just go to bed and keep Billie happy."

"Billie can go screw herself."

He was sufficiently rattled to lose naturally for the next hour or so, and Emma announced that she wanted a rest. But there was a commotion at this, and Rick seemed to think she was treating him with contempt.

"I can wipe the table with any of you . . . do you think I'm a fifty dollars a week sucker . . . come on, what are you, a hundred bucks up and you want to go to bed . . . this isn't bingo night in Boston, you know . . . sit down and shut up."

Emma sat down and took ten thousand dollars from him. And the commotion had served a double purpose, because the game at the other table had broken off temporarily while they all came over to watch Rick losing his manhood. And a few minutes later Billie came down in her nightdress to watch and scold. Curt Krystal sensed a pleasurable humiliation and he stood behind Emma for the rest of the game. The players remained icily calm, but the spectators were whipping themselves up into a frenzy, of one kind or another.

"If you ruin us, Rick, husband mine, I'll walk on you with the first man who shows me his wallet. . . ."

"Shut up, you cow." Rick was looking at his fellow players for mercy—somebody had to be cheating, and didn't they know this? couldn't they object? But nobody objected. "Five hundred dollars," he bidded.

"Have you got five hundred dollars?" It was half past five. At half past seven the tension had grown more hostile, and Krystal thought that Rick was ruined. "Work it out, because we aren't used to being bilked. Work it out, lad."

Rick stared glassily at him, scarcely seeing, and then slowly, like an automaton he laid his two return air tickets on the table.

Two heavyweights from Chicago dragged Billie from the room to prevent her abuse from spoiling concentration. Emma dealt him two fives. She dealt Albert Bein a king and a two, and he quickly won. He spread out his cards on the table with a gold studded smile, leant back and lit a cigar, looking like Clark Gable in a western film. "I guess," he drawled lazily, "this is where you start walking."

Emma watched the shattered youth stumble to his feet. He groped his way blindly to the drinks and poured out a massive Scotch. It had taken nine hours to ruin him, and she felt a surge of pity—he was so good looking, so young. The idea of breaking him was clever, in the abstract, but there was something terrible in seeing him broken. He was isolated now from the rest, and it was a distance that even hysteria wouldn't bridge.

"Surely," Al murmured, "there's no point in stopping the game now?" The mood had caught on.

Rick leaned towards him and shook his head, like a drunken man. "What do you want, my life or something? I'm cleaned out. I'll have to sell my home to pay these bills. I'll have to sell everything." He drank another tumbler of Scotch, as if he was thirsty. "What can I play for? Even my rackets will be taken away from me now. I'm nobody."

"Don't be downhearted, Rick," said the soothing voice of Curt Krystal. "You have a beautiful wife."

Albert Bein blew out a cloud of smoke. "Now that's poker," he drawled.

Rick shuddered, but Emma knew from his eyes that he was going to fall for it. "What do you think I am?"

"Ten thousand. Dollars." Krystal took the cards from Emma as if to declare the game over. "We were only trying to help."

Rick waved him back to the table and sat down himself with the bottle of whisky beside him. "I'll deal," he said tensely. Then with a defiant glare at Emma, "So what have I got to lose?" And twelve people chuckled encouragingly.

The cards were dealt, two to each player, and Rick dealt himself a ten and a jack. Emma sat out, because what would she want with a fluffy girl in the yellow-teddy bear belt? Curt Krystal was the only person who might beat Rick, if he knew that the next card to be turned up was an ace.

Rick was as ashen faced as a man can be without his heart stopping. He watched the other players turn up their cards as if he was watching his life tossed away. And they were laughing, that made it worse. It was all a hilarious game to these strangers. He watched Krystal lean forward and reach with a pudgy hand for the next card. Rick had lost.

"Oh God." Rick buried his head in his hands.

If all gamblers secretly want to lose, Emma reflected, he must feel very happy.

Krystal eased himself out of the chair and padded across to the door. "There is no such thing as a frigid woman," he said softly. Then he went and closed the door behind him. The people left in the room were grinning fatuously, not knowing what to say and embarrassed at Rick's presence. There was a silence of nearly two endless minutes, and then a scream cut through the house.

Billie was screaming desperately upstairs.

It was a signal to Rick, and he hauled himself to his feet. "You bastards," he shouted. "You can't ruin me so easily. I know too much to be ruined. I'll tell everybody about that Russian clit, I'll tell them who put her up to this little game. Do you want everyone to know she's being smuggled into America?" His face was red again now, and he shouted hysterically, "I could earn fifty thousand for this story!"

"What," asked a deep feminine voice behind him, "is the matter?" It was Tamara, standing in the doorway with all the authority of a stern mother. "Have you gone mad, Rick?"

"He lost all his money," Emma explained.

"It was that clit of a dealer, she stacked the cards!" Rick suddenly advanced on Emma with his whisky bottle at the ready. "Why did you do it to me?" he asked, almost pleadingly. Then he lunged at her head.

Emma seized his arm with both hands, thrust her leg behind him and slapped him to the floor. It was the reverse bent arm lock, and Tamara applauded knowledgeably. Rick stayed on the floor nursing a damaged shoulder, sniffling occasionally, muttering to himself in Italian.

"You must be Emma Peel," she said regally. "I like a woman to be cruel. We shall enjoy each other. Did Curt tell you you're staying with me until I leave the country?"

"No," said Emma. "He's been busy all night with man's talk."

"Men are bores. Listen to that vulgar lout taking his pleasure. Shall we go upstairs and I'll show you the way about." Tamara picked up Rick by the collar and bundled him across the room into Albert's lap with the instruction to take care of the baby. Then she took Emma by the hand and led her away.

11

Steed waited until the afternoon and then rang Emma again. There was still no answer from her flat. Oh well, she was probably too busy enjoying herself; maybe she had forgotten; the line might have been engaged. He had a glass of milk while he debated with himself for another ten minutes, and then he decided that she needed tracing. That's the trouble with young women, he thought wearily, they always need looking after.

He took an old fashioned cigarette lighter from the bottom of his case and sat by the open window. It was a miniature radio and the wick pulled out to become an aerial, the wavelength was set by the screw at the bottom, and the arm thing that snuffs out the flame was the transmitter contact. Steed prayed nobody would come in and find him fooling with these damned gimmicks. Why Thorburn couldn't have a telephone installed in that derelict house he couldn't imagine. It was the Boy Scout training that did it, learning semaphore and leaving track signs scrawled all over the pavement. And Steed could never remember the morse code anyway.

It took him half an hour to establish that she had gone off on Friday night with three car loads of Americans and had not been seen again. Steed tapped out his thanks and promised Thorburn a bottle of meths for Christmas. Then he put the contraption away. Perhaps his attitude was reactionary, he reflected; after all, if he had cast his principles aside and put a homing device on Emma he would have less difficulty now in finding her.

Steed made three phone calls putting men onto Curt Krystal's known haunts and then set off for London. Alf travelled beside him and the man from M.I.5 trailed behind. The Bentley was fitted with a supercharged 1966 Rolls Royce engine, slightly modified, and the sight of his 1929 rhinoceros doing eighty miles an hour down the motorway excited disbelief in the drivers he passed.

Just outside Luton he stopped and made three

more phone calls. Krystal had a house in Golders Green but it had been empty since Friday. The chartered plane had landed at Rochford and it was still there, expecting to return to Chicago on Monday. And no party of Americans had been seen in any of the bigger London clubs.

Another modern tendency that Steed disliked was the use of gratuitous violence. He preferred to have no part of it. "Alf," he said thoughtfully, "I'd like you to deal with someone for me."

Alf was cautious. "How big is he?"

"About your size, but he's older than you are."

Steed turned off the main road and went down the deserted lane towards Sloman woods. After a few minutes he drew up beside the bridle path that led through the trees into the heart of the forest. He paused to make sure that hatchet face was following, then he took a rope and a crowbar from the boot of the car and gave them to Alf to carry. "Now, come with me and make as much noise as possible," said Steed.

Alf was a city man at heart, and the naked branches, frozen soil, the different browns and blacks of the forest in winter had no magic for him. He was more concerned with the cold, and the gasps of white breath so sharply visible, the murmur of icy wind, set him chattering about bleedin' eskimos. But they carried on, past occasional drifts of snow and over brittle swamps until they reached a sudden chalk pit.

"You see, Alf, the romance of the English countryside. I used to play in this wood thirty odd years ago, and it hasn't changed."

"Well you have," Alf observed sullenly. "What do we do now?"

"Play." Steed took the rope from behind him and ran a loop from the edge of the pit to a tree whose branches stretched overhead. Then he covered over the loop with dead, wet leaves. "The idea is to wait until our victim is standing in this loop and then pull it tight; with any luck he ends up, upside down, suspended from this branch. And if it doesn't work, well at least the chap will be thoroughly unnerved."

Steed tied the rope to the branch while Alf warmed himself with the iron bar, hewing out several square feet of chalk from the pit face beneath the ace where Valentine Dyall was meant to stand. It was quickly done, and then they waited.

"Why does this geezer keep following you?" Alf asked after a few moments.

"I wish I knew."

"You must have some idea what's going on, Mr. S."

"Only vaguely. Someone is getting at the British government and the higher ranks of the civil service by using up-to-date methods of brainwashing. But I'm not sure who that someone is; it might be Russia or America, or rather the Mafia. And one reason it's difficult to get to the bottom of all this is that M.I.5 are in there playing a game of their own."

Alf scratched his head. "I thought you were one of them."

"I'm not in the same department." Steed smiled wryly. "Healthy competition, you know, like school houses and different regiments." Alf looked blank, as well he might. "These rivalries get pretty rough sometimes."

There was a shout from across the pit, and Steed saw the man in black tumble forward as the ground gave way under him, then his feet caught up in the noose and he swung neatly upside down. A beautiful operation, and Steed beamed proudly at Alf Knight.

"Now let's go and talk to the fellow. And remember, it might be necessary for you to persuade him."

The man's wallet, cigarette lighter and a gun had fallen to the ground. Steed picked them up and went through the wallet. "What's your name?" Steed asked him. He could see from the driving license that it was Pinkerton, but it was best to start with the easy questions.

"You'll pay for this, Steed. I'll see that you get ten years for assault."

"Threatened assault," Steed corrected him. His head was about level with Pinkerton's head the other way up, although of course Pinkerton's head was getting redder. "Before the evening is finished I expect you to tell me exactly why you've been following me around, why I was told to keep out of London, how M.I.5 comes into this and precisely what you've learned. Start as soon as you like."

"I have no intention of telling you anything," said Pinkerton.

Alf tugged his forelock, said sorry guv, and

thumped the man in the kidneys with the crowbar. He screamed, but he didn't start talking. "No, Alf, really!" Steed protested. "Couldn't you be a little more subtle? I know you're doing your best, but perhaps we could strip him of his clothes and then pour cold water over him. Much more civilised than this vulgar brutality, and in this weather it might be effective."

Alf was less put out than Steed expected, and he began removing Pinkerton's heavy overcoat with enthusiasm. Pinkerton struggled and yelled, but Alf managed to make a neat pile of clothes on the ground before he was stopped by a problem in logic. How do you remove trousers and pants when the ankles are trussed together?

"Make a bundle of them round his feet," Steed advised.

"I'm afraid it'll ruin the creases, guv."

"That's the price of being a hero," said Steed.

Alf had to climb back up to the top of the pit. By the time Pinkerton was effectively stripped, hanging like a side of meat in a butcher's shop, his flesh was turning a bluish grey and his teeth were vibrating audibly. He was a scraggy man and the goose pimples made him look even more unattractive. Alf returned with several rusty cans filled with slushy snow.

"Just think of this as a sauna bath, sir." Alf slapped the soggy snow over Pinkerton's stomach and watched it slither down his thin chest. "It's not what you might call clean, but it works just as well."

"I'll die . . . help . . . oh God!"

After a few more cans of icy wet snow Pinkerton was ready to talk. Alf was almost disappointed, but he accepted the moral, that violence wasn't the answer to everything. He cut Pinkerton down and helped him on with his clothes.

"You'll be able to move again soon," Steed reassured him. "You need a hot bath and a warm bed. Why not get the conversation over with so that you can book into a first class hotel?"

"What do you want to know?" Pinkerton stammered.

"Was Smeck-Hudson a security leak?"

"No. We got back all his papers as soon as he went off the rails. That's all I know. I've been following you around because that was my assignment; I don't know why they wanted you out of the way. Something's going on, but I don't know what."

"Lies," said Steed.

Alf picked up the crowbar.

"Fletcher knows all about it, he's master-minding this case. Why don't you ask him?"

"You can ask him, sweetheart." Steed pulled the shivering shadow to his feet and pushed him towards the bridal path. "You'll telephone Fletcher and say that I've slipped you. Tell him you know that Curt Krystal has something I want back and so I'll be with him."

They went a few miles and booked Pinkerton into the Royal Hotel near Watford. Steed gave the barman detailed instructions on how to make the hot punch. He hadn't realised that he was freezing as well. But the heavy warmth of the hotel made him feel suddenly tired.

"Stop yawning, Alf. We've a busy night ahead of us."

They sat in the lounge beside Pinkerton and listened to his explanation on the telephone. "Yes, sir, I'm sorry, sir. But if we know where Curt Krystal is spending the weekend we can easily pick him up again . . . Oh. Yes, sir, I see."

Pinkerton hung up gloomily. "We don't know where Krystal hangs out." He sipped the hot punch. "He has a secret hide-out somewhere near the coast, near Brighton it seems, but we don't know where because until now we've never needed to find out."

Steed sighed. "I suppose that's something. How do you find the punch?"

"Do you know what Fletcher said?" He laughed cynically, until tears ran down his face and he was exhausted. "He said you aren't dangerous. He said you're a happy innocent who's heading for trouble, that's all. Not dangerous. . . ."

Steed finished his punch and led Alf back out into the night.

Emma knew that she was a prisoner here. But she was so exhausted after the marathon game of poker that she slept until eight o'clock the following evening. In her half-waking moments she remembered that Steed would be worrying because she hadn't rung him, and in her dreams she argued that it was impossible to ring him anyway, and then the problem would swirl off into the distance, she was asleep again.

The bed was a sybaritic four poster, and across the room was an open range fire that blazed comfortingly all day. Once when she half awoke and saw snow on the dead oak in the grounds she imagined she was a small girl again in bed with measles, but something was wrong and soon she remembered what it was—she was twenty years older.

She really woke up when she felt a hand moving across her stomach. There was some giggling going on, and as she opened her eyes Emma had the hallucinatory experience of seeing two Chinese faces grinning at her from the foot of the bed. The hand belonged to the third Chinese girl, who seemed to be giving a lecture on anatomy to her compatriots.

"What on earth are you doing?" Emma demanded.

They nudged each other and tittered. "In our country," one of them managed to explain, "we have a legend about white women. . . ."

Well, at least they were friendly.

Emma shooed them out of the room and then went across the landing to have a bath. This was the sort of home, so splendidly remote in the old Sussex countryside, that Emma felt completely relaxed in, if only the details weren't so wrong. She lay back in the steaming water and listened to the fifteen men cart-horsing around the house. The Fenjal smelled perfect as the water lapped sensuously round her body. Yes, the only trouble with absolute luxury was the other people who could also afford it.

She looked out of the window while she dried herself vigorously with a towel. There was a thick blanket of snow on the ground from two weeks ago and Emma felt an overwhelming desire to run naked into the garden and roll in a deep snowdrift. Her blood was tingling with life, and the icy temperature somehow added to her sense of exhilaration.

But when she came out of the bathroom Krystal was waiting for her.

"Hi," he said with a brave wave of his hand. "You look great. How was the bed?"

"Great," said Emma. "I think Queen Elizabeth must have slept well when she stayed here."

"Are you hungry?" He took Emma by the arm and led her into the dining room. He was suspiciously relaxed and friendly. "The others are having sandwiches sent into them. Don't want to waste good playing time." He laughed indulgently and pulled out a chair for her to sit at the head of a massive table. "Food!" he yelled.

It was a superbly period dining room, surprisingly simple in line and heavy with wooden beams, large mahogany cupboards and an oak tiled floor. Krystal lowered his body into a chair at the other end of the table, fifteen feet away. "You'll enjoy this," he bawled, "it's an old American dish called Spanish fried chicken. I don't know why it's called Spanish."

An aged retainer who must have come with the house brought in the casserole, and it smelled good. He poured Emma a glass of Jamaican Long and then served the food. Strips of ham, onion and tomatoes, and unidentifiable herbs as well as the pieces of chicken. Emma tasted and pronounced the meal delicious.

"Just to show that hamburgers and hot dogs aren't the only dishes to come out of America. By the way, this room was renovated by an American designer!"

"I don't need to be persuaded," she called. "I admire Louis Armstrong and Allen Ginsberg, Kazen, Norbert Wiener. . . ."

"You'd like America."

"I'm sure I would, that's why I don't want to go there. Every English person I know who's once been to America has wanted desperately to go and live there."

"We'll arrange for you to make a trip." Krystal was grinning extravagantly in an effort to crease his face into amiability.

"You're a patriot," Emma said uneasily. She felt that he might be serious about sending her to America.

"Of course," said Krystal. "Do you think it strange that a social undesirable should be patriotic? It's America that doesn't approve of me, not the other way about. You always find that gaols are full of intensely nationalistic people, and they're what you call conservative."

"Yes, I suppose I should have known."

"The Mafia saved thousands of lives when America invaded Italy in 1944. We let Lucky Luciano out of prison and he organised the whole landing, he went with the first Americans and negotiated directly with Don Calo. Mussolini's army didn't stand a chance against the patriotism of the Mafia."

"The honoured society," murmured Emma. "How do you join?"

Krystal laughed. "I've already enrolled you as a member. After last night's exhibition I couldn't let you masquerade as a law-abiding woman."

Emma gulped at the Jamaican Long and the rum caught the back of her throat.

"That was the most dishonest hundred grand that I've ever seen a woman earn, and it was done with real English style. The others are still wondering how you managed it." Krystal obviously found it the biggest joke since Al Capone was imprisoned for a tax irregularity. "But they'll never know, because I destroyed the deck."

"How did you know?"

"I'm a professional. Don't look so amazed, Emma, it stood to reason. And how else would I have known to turn up that ace to finish Rick?" The table was shaking with his laughter and Emma tried to look equally amused. "Only thing that bothers me," he said eventually, "is why you did it. Why Rick?"

"I needed the money."

"I hope so." He nodded seriously. "Poor Rick. I never saw a man so cleaned out. I had to give him a hundred dollars before he left to make his way in the world."

Emma laughed. "Do you think he'll become president of the United States?"

"He has as much chance as anybody else."

Half an hour later Krystal heaved himself up from

the table. "Shall we join the ladies?" He took Emma's arm again and led her into the lounge where Tamara was relaxing with her three Chinese playmates. "Tamara has taken to you in a big way, Emma. She wants to take you away from me."

Tamara Petrova was transformed. During the day she had bobbed her hair so that it looked the height of Beatle fashion and it was parted on the right. She wore no make-up, and the navy blue trouser suit was the final touch in converting her into a stunningly handsome man. Emma had to remind herself that Tamara was a buxom woman, because she almost didn't flinch when Tamara kissed her on both cheeks.

"Darling," she said like Charles Boyer, "has Curt told you about our plans for you?"

Curt Krystal said something about getting round to it and poured himself a drink. "We were busy eating." He clattered the ice into the glass with masculine clumsiness; Tamara watched him distastefully. "Yea, we talked about America and the Cosa Nostra. It was a good dinner."

"You enjoy your dinner too much, Curt. Your mind softens at the meal table and you talk always about the Mafia or about power. Like when you are drunk you talk about yourself and Mussolini. 'I am indestructible,' you shout. Poor Curt. You can never forget that you're Sicilian."

Curt grinned idiotically at Emma and said that he never argued with a jealous woman, if you'll forgive the word. Then he left and took his drink with him.

"You mustn't mind Curt, darling, he's boring, that's all. A little stupid, as all men must be who seek after power. I think Napoleon must have been a tedious bed-fellow and Tamburlaine was a cretin. A little lop-sided, eh?"

"Do you mean," Emma asked, retreating to the sofa, "that you are nothing to do with his quest for power?"

"Well, only indirectly. I am a scientist, and Curt has a mystical faith in science to bestow absolute power. Just as Earl Haig thought that he could win the first war with God on his side so Curt imagines that he can conquer the world with science on his side. But as Earl Haig found, you also need intelligence."

"I'm a bit unintelligent myself," said Emma, moving away from Tamara's romantic pats. "What is he trying to achieve?"

The look that Tamara gave her made Emma freeze for a moment, because its absolute ruthlessness and calculation was quite separate from the obvious physical attraction that Tamara also felt. "He's dabbling in politics, darling. The Mafia has never been able to resist political dabbling, and now it seems to be playing with international affairs. Out of sheer patriotism, of course. They seem to think that Britain is going communist—gradually, with its Labour Party and its welfare state and the decline of the class structure, so the simple idiots who run the Mafia decided to discredit the government, undermine public morale and stampede the country into a right wing reaction."

So that was it; that was why Tamara had been so deliberately clumsy in leading Smeck-Hudson astray and so obvious in her spy role. But it was also it, because they couldn't allow Emma to wander abroad knowing this. "What are these plans you have for me?"

"Will you marry me?"

"No." Emma stood up indignantly and pointed to the black leather jacket and the slimma slacks she was wearing. "People will think we're homosexuals." At which the three little maids from school collapsed in helpless laughter.

"Darling, don't be a prude. We're going to America together, as man and wife." Emma, of course, as the wife. It seemed that Tamara was expert as passing for a man, and poor dear Rick's passport was being adapted to enable them to return to the U.S.A. with the jet set gamblers. "You see, my love, I'm likely to be arrested if I stay in this country, and you are likely to be killed. So we are leaving tomorrow. I hope," she whispered, "we shall be very happy together."

Steed sat looking out across the English Channel. He couldn't see the sea, but he could hear its surprisingly noisy roar, and from the crashing of the waves he judged it to be high tide. Far out beyond the three mile limit were the lights of a ship moving imperceptibly towards the Atlantic. And behind them, further along the promenade, was the noise of a beat group in a pub sending its mating call into the night.

"I suppose," Steed said as a last resort, "Krystal didn't give you his change of address?"

Alf was outraged. "What me, guv? Wotchermean? I ain't got nothing to do with him now! How should I know where he is?"

"No, all right." Steed felt as a general must feel when he hazards the lives of his men in a necessary (to the general) gamble. But Alf was his only lead to Krystal and so the chance had to be taken. "We're wasting our time," he said to Alf, "you might as well go back to London."

"What about you, guv?"

"I'll potter about down here until tomorrow. But I want you to catch the eleven o'clock train back to Victoria." He took a five pound note from his wallet and gave it to Alf, "to cover your expenses."

Steed watched the villainous little man shuffle off towards the station. Poor old Alf. Steed lit a panatella and waited. There was fifteen minutes to wait. Alf was too trusting, that was his trouble, he assumed he was the only crook in an honest world. But Steed resolved to look after him during the next few hours.

Fifteen minutes later Steed cruised up to the station and parked in the forecourt. He didn't have to wait long this time. At five minutes to eleven he saw Alf coming back out of the station between two very large men. Alf was arguing volubly but his escort didn't seem interested. They bundled him into a Cadillac and drove away. They didn't see Steed.

Generals have to do things like that, using a knight as bait, putting a phone call through to the Mississippi to draw the gangsters out of their hideout.

Luckily the Cadillac was entirely unsuitable for Brighton's average-size streets, and the motorists of southern England were crowding out from the pubs and cinemas to make speed even more impossible. Steed followed easily and unobtrusively for about ten miles, and then the Cadillac swung off the main road.

Steed turned out his lights and followed blindly after the red tail lamps. They went through a tiny village and on for about a mile, then the red tail lamps went out. The Cadillac had stopped. Steed stopped as well.

They were taking Alf into a huge, renovated place that Steed expected to be converted into a hotel and called The Old Barn. But it was a house, and the men's accents confirmed that it belonged to Curt Krystal. Steed waited for the party to go inside and settle before he circled round to the back of the place and clambered over the wall.

Apart from the fact that he could see no sign of Alf Knight there was nothing abnormal about the house party. Steed watched fourteen Americans playing poker for very high stakes. Emma Peel was in a room at the side of the house, relaxing with a glamorous young man whom Steed assumed to be a pop singer, but whom he quickly placed as Tamara Petrova in drag. So where was Curt Krystal, he wondered.

Steed decided on disruptive action, which required the use of a telephone, and the last one he had noticed was a mile back. But there was time.

Steed ambled leisurely back to the car and went into the village. A large brandy in the Prince of Wales and the use of the telephone.

"Hello, is that the police?" Steed asked in a deplorable American accent. "My name is Krystal and I live at the Old Barn, a mile out on Sandy Lane. Can you send a few men out to pick up a burglar I've caught breaking into my house—his name is Alfred Knight."

It worked. The station sergeant called him General and promised to send a car immediately. Steed drawled his thanks out of the side of his mouth and finished the brandy. He could see in the mirror over the bar that he was being watched, by a swarthy young man who used too much hair oil. The young man followed him out of the pub and climbed into the Bentley beside him.

"Don't let's have any argument," said the new friend, "I've got a gun pointing straight at your gut."

A rather typical young-executive's-wife followed them and sat in the back seat. She looked the talkative type, but she didn't say anything; she was too tense, although Steed guessed that once she started his problems were over.

"My name's Rick Montalbain. Who are you?"

"Steed, John Steed. My pleasure." Steed put out his hand, but Rick wasn't fooled. "Are you a hitch-hiker or something?"

"Cut out the gags, I was listening to that phone call. Why did you say your name was Krystal?"

"Well, it's a long and complex story, but as you have the advantage I suppose I have the time. By the way, I presume you're the fifteenth American? I wondered where the other was. Taking a breath of evening air? These week-end parties can be a strain, the way they coop people up together, and really there isn't anywhere much to go, is there?"

"We aren't talking about my problems. Just answer the question."

Steed chuckled confidentially and pressed the starter. "To be perfectly honest, I was just trying to cause a little trouble for Krystal. He's an old friend of mine—"

"Where are you going, buddy boy?"

"Back to the Old Barn. Right?"

"Wrong. Stay put and carry on talking."

"All right. Is your wife comfortable back there? Yes, Krystal is a man with a few scores to settle, and I was preparing to settle them. I gather you feel some resentment of him yourself?"

"You can say that again," said the wife.

"Shut up, Billie."

"Can't we just take this bum's money and clear out? Let him fix Krystal, it doesn't matter to you. We need the car more than a friendly chew over old friends. Come on—"

"Shut up!"

"Who are you telling to shut up, you bum? You can't treat me like this any more because you're just nothing, you know that? You never were anything except a loud mouthed bank account, and now you're through. I don't have to listen to the big talk any more—"

Rich made the mistake of leaning over the back of

his seat to slap her face, and during that moment of domestic endeavour Steed hit him on the base of the skull with the gun he had confiscated from Pinkerton. Rick slumped back against the dashboard.

"Sorry about that, but he was being difficult," said Steed as he tied Rick's hands to his ankles. "Can I buy you a drink? You look as if you need one."

Steed listened to her grievances for half an hour, and by that time he had lost sympathy with her. But he pieced the story together, and by closing time was happy to return Billie to her groggy but disarmed husband. It seemed that Emma had been up to her Peel again. And so not unnaturally they wanted to get her out of the country. Steed would have felt the same, he decided.

"What does your husband do?" Steed asked.

"He's in the fruit business, importing and all."

It was an old story. "You mean he's a Mafia boss and that's his front. Well, he'll have to work for a living now."

"What," Billie asked as he climbed back into his Bentley, "do you do?"

"I'm a politician."

Billie looked shocked. One of them; socialised medicine and national assistance. She helped her husband out of the car and stood him clear while Steed started up the engine. "What party do you stand for?"

"That depends," said Steed, "on the time of day. At eleven o'clock I'm usually pretty right wing. But I get almost socialist by lunch time. It's something to do with my physical well-being. The only occasions when I feel really certain are when I'm talking to people who have rigid views; I always disagree with them."

"What me, a burglar? Cor-krisse, you people got one-track minds. You ask Mr. K.— go on, ask him! Mr. Krystal, guv, do I look like a burglar? See, I got five quid in my pocket, so why should I—?"

"Keep quiet," snapped the sergeant. "I'm sorry, Mr. Krystal, but do I understand that you didn't ring the police?"

"Correct," said Krystal. "This man is known to me, and he came here for perfectly honest reasons."

"See! I ask you, me a bleedin' burglar."

"Keep quiet."

"I'm sorry you've been misled, sergeant, but you can safely leave Mr. Knight with me."

Alf Knight suddenly dropped the outrage. "Yes, well, I don't mind coming down to the station and making a statement. I mean, you've got your job to do, haven't you?"

"Keep quiet."

Emma watched the scene in complete bewilderment. She recognised Steed's small friend, but she couldn't understand how the police had come into it. For a few minutes she'd thought that the F.B.I. had moved in to arrest its finest collection of top criminals since 1949. But then Alf Knight had reduced the whole occasion to farce.

Curt Krystal went to the front door with the sergeant while Alf remained in the lounge looking pleadingly from face to face. But the Americans all started back stonily and only Tamara smiled.

"Tsu Ming," said Krystal when he returned, "this man is too much trouble. Kill him."

Nobody moved, and nobody spoke. They all watched Alf struggling to understand his death sentence. They seemed to find it absorbing. Then as Tsu Ming got to her feet Alf started to react. Incoherently he begged them to let him off, promised and pleaded. As Tsu Ming came towards him he burst into tears and whined on one long, low note. Tsu Ming paused in front of him and bowed ceremonially. Alf sank to his knees.

Krystal was grinning broadly.

And Emma dared not intervene. They were suspicious enough of her already. She tensed her lips. He was on their side anyway.

The whine ceased abruptly and Alf was stretching upwards, veins standing out on his scarlet face. He seemed to be reaching up in agony, and Tsu Ming held him in that posture with a three-finger grip on his spinal column until it snapped and he fell back onto the floor. He never made a sound, but he floundered for a bit like a fish on a river bank. That was a hold they leave out of the handy judo manuals.

"Now," said Krystal, "I guess a spot of hunting might be appropriate, to round out the evening."

Aw jeez—hunting what—haven't we wasted enough time?

"You guys aren't very bright tonight," Krystal purred icily. "The man who tipped us off that Alf was in Brighton obviously did so because he wanted to follow Hank and Steve back to this house. When he found out where we were he sent the law in to rescue his stooge. Is that sense? This guy Steed thinks good sense, I've decided, but he still behaves idiotically. He's out there in the grounds and we've got to go out with our guns and have a spot of winter sports."

"See here, Curt, the guy's your problem—"

Krystal was chillingly authoritative, and Emma realised why he had been given the European network. He was a born leader of men. He walked into the centre of the room and glared at the dead body on the floor. "Are you thugs as soft as you look? Is gambling all you're fit for now? Okay, so play cards if that's your level and I'll make Britain safe for you by myself. I haven't forgotten the way I came up."

He held his audience in suspense while he poured a Black Hand Bourbon for himself. "I came up the same way as you guys, with a gun and a steel nerve and more brains than the guys who are dead now. An I can still use my gun—I haven't lost my nerve. You men may have spent so long with your string of dolls' houses and your dope rings that you've forgotten. But you'll remember someday that you got where you are by being tough, and that was the way you should have stayed—tough and at the top."

Aw chuck it—okay, we'll have your man hunt—I can still hit a man at sixty yards in the dark—so who is this guy?

The idea caught on pretty rapidly, and soon they reminded Emma of a Sunday morning meet outside the George & Dragon, with the baying of hounds and the thought of the fox creating a mood of bloody anticipation. They cracked a few jokes and told the women to stay by the Christmas tree until they came back with the bastard.

Emma watched through her bedroom window, and from time to time she saw a shadow flit across the lawn. Once a shot rang out, but nothing happened. Then she caught sight of Steed on the roof of the east wing, outlined against the frosty stars. The fool. He was taking risks, annoyed, she assumed, by what had happened to Alf. He was sometimes too human to be a good undercover man.

"Do you know him?" asked Tamara's voice behind her.

"No, but I always sympathise with the underdog. That man is outnumbered fifteen to one."

"You shoot him," Tamara instructed.

"They said it was man's work. And apart from that, I don't take orders from you."

"We're going to be married—"

"So don't treat me as Al Capone would treat a lieutenant he suspected of going straight. It makes you boring. . . ."

A voice in the garden shouted, "On the roof," as Steed was easing his way visibly round the chimney stack, and a volley of gun shots replied instantly. Emma saw him fall more than fifty feet to a chorus of excited cheers. He didn't move after that, until Curt Krystal dragged him by the feet into the house.

12

John Steed fell down and down through a bottomless black shaft, and his brain swirled painfully into oblivion. It might have been days or an eternity later when he heard Curt Krystal's voice saying, "He's alive. Keep quiet while I bring him round." It was reassuring to have a second opinion, because Steed didn't feel very much alive.

"We've got a plane to catch, man. We believe you know how to brainwash him."

"A simple demonstration," Krystal purred. "After all, you are the shareholders, my colleagues in this operation."

Steed blinked his eyes open and found a circle of faces peering down at him, expressionless eyes behind rimless spectacles and bloodshot eyes that seemed not to see, piggy eyes buried in pink flesh and eyes invisible behind dark glasses. . . . He tried to move, and couldn't. Death would be something like this, cold and paralysed and impersonal in a badly lit cellar—the only light brilliantly focused on the corpse's face. "Is this a morgue?" Steed asked.

"It's all right," Krystal reassured him, "you're in my laboratory."

"I thought I was dead."

"A graze across the temple as you fell, from a bullet that each of us claims, and luckily you fell into the rhododendron bushes. You'll live, Mr. Steed, for another thirty years, although you'll never be quite the same again."

"Why can't I move?"

Krystal chuckled. "You're strapped to the operating table." He pressed a button and the table rose at an angle so that Steed could see the rest of his body. It looked intact. "We have to take precautions, because you'll soon be undergoing a pretty rigorous course of treatment. And of course somebody might try to help you. Maybe. But if a certain young lady *is* working with you it's small consolation, because she'll be in Chicago by tonight."

"Which young lady is that?"

"Never mind." He leered. "She's been claimed as war booty."

Steed tried to suppress his smile. Emma was not made of the stuff of the Trojan women. Or by God he hoped not.

The room was oddly shaped, with its ceiling curling down at one end into the wall so that it resembled an umbrella with Steed inside the centre; and at the other end of the room was a selection of electrical devices, wires and instrument panels. It was all hideously scientific. There was also a massive tank of water that would be ideal for anybody who wanted to keep pet sharks.

"We'll never be in Chicago tonight if we hang around watching you do your job," said the one in dark glasses. "I'll leave you to it." The others muttered agreement and returned upstairs.

"Okay," said Krystal sadly, "send down the Chinese girls." He turned back and bent over Steed. "They don't attach much importance to you, Mr. Steed. But I do. Within three days you'll be going back to Brawhill a changed man, and we shall be friends. I want to be friends. After all, what's to be gained from enmity?"

"What's to be gained from our friendship?"

"We shall improve Anglo-American relations, Mr. Steed."

Steed sighed. There was no point in trying to pretend any more. "I know, you want me to undermine British morale. But surely to do that you need publicity, preferably from a big trial? So why are you sending Madame Petrova off to America? Surely that won't boost the kind of security scandal you're trying to create?"

Krystal shook his head. "It was part of our agreement. But only you and I know where she is going. To everyone else she will simply have disappeared, maybe back to Russia. Isn't that good enough? The people will say your pinko government can't even arrest its spies when it reads about them in the papers."

The three Chinese girls came into the cellar prepared for business. They were dressed in judo-gi uniforms again. Steed smiled at them in welcome; why be nervous? if their names had been Miss Jones, Miss

Brown and Miss Tidmarsh he wouldn't have turned a hair! It was a childish prejudice against the yellow peril. Well, that was what he told himself. They didn't smile back, but orientals don't smile much.

"Okay, kids, give him the usual routine, but make it a few grades tougher than usual. I also want to know who he's working for, what they know and what they're after. Apart from that, just carry on with the treatment. Okay? I'll be upstairs if you need me."

"I'm quite prepared to tell you what the British government knows," Steed called after him. "I'll tell you now. It might make you decide to leave on the plane from Rochford with your friends."

"There are procedures, Mr. Steed. You will talk when my girls have done their work. Why do you think I employ them?" He left the room with a jocular wag of his podgy forefinger.

"My name is Shin Peng," said one of the girls. "Shall we begin now?" She fetched a bamboo rod from a cupboard in the corner. "This we call in China a bastinado. It causes great pain without breaking the skin. Except first it will be necessary for Tsu Ming to bare your back and thighs. Do not worry, she will do it with complete impersonality."

Tsu Ming removed his jacket, shirt and vest with the expertise of a trained nurse giving a blanket bath, adjusting the leather bonds and then replacing them without giving Steed a chance to break loose. As she turned him over Steed was surprised to find that he was very weak from the incident in the grounds.

"And now Kuei-ying will apply the bastinado. She is most expert. Her name means Gentle Sorrow."

The pleasures of this kind of thing always seemed improbable when it started. Steed winced and squirmed under the stinging swishes of the cane across his back, and he waited to cross the threshold into more positive response. He listened to the whistling sound and the sharp smack against flesh. Relax! It used to be known as a spanking good time. He told himself that the burning cuts would soon transmute themselves into a pleasurably erotic glow of flesh and sexuality. But it hurt! Relax, and pretend to enjoy it. Perhaps you need to have a thing about Chinese girls. He concentrated on developing a thing about Chinese girls. They were neat, compact, and they meant well. "I've already—agreed, for Christ's sake, to talk!"

Shin Peng ran a hand across his brow, but the burning blows continued. "We continue for the recognised period, Mr. Steed. It has to be that way. This is the art in China." The oriental bitch, she was being bloody British about it all.

Emma gathered from the way they were speaking among themselves that Steed was still alive. But she also knew that he would need help pretty quickly if it were to be much use. Those girls weren't just ordinary playmates.

"Darling, have you seen our passport? We look like the ideal couple." Tamara showed her the adapted passport they had taken from Rick. "I must say it makes you look hard, but perhaps that's as it should be. You look like a reformed spiv. But my gentle expression balances for you. Am I not handsome? We must remember to be Rick and Billie from now until we reach Chicago."

The Americans were all placing their bets on the hundred mile race to Rochford. They had allowed two hours to reach the airport, and the six-to-four favourite was Krystal's kandy koloured tangerine thing, because even though Curt was staying behind his chauffeur knew southern England better than anyone else. And you can't beat an American car when other things are equal.

The farewells didn't take long, because their minds were on other things, such as watching Emma to make sure she didn't try to slip away, and setting off a minute early to gain an advantage. The only consolation was that Tamara and the chauffeur would be alone with Emma in the car, and that hunded mile ride would present her best chance to escape.

"Goodbye, my dear," said Krystal. "I had you marked down as being mine, and I shall always regret that we never made love. Think of me sometimes when you are enjoying America with Tamara." Krystal seemed almost sincere, and his handshake was that of a lover. He kissed her on both cheeks. "We shall never see each other again."

"I'm sure we shall," said Emma. "Au revoir."

They sped off at something like sixty miles an hour along the narrow lane and through the village. They almost played bumper cars, and when they came to the main road Emma's chauffeur edged a pursuing Daimler into a Keep Left sign. Emma was surprised. His ears still kept up the peaked cap and his head went straight down into his collar, but he seemed more interested in the race than last time. Tamara must have bribed him.

The ride to London was one of the most dangerously expert she had ever experienced off the race track. The driver's short cuts and back wheel skids were an aesthetic pleasure to see and a chilling fright to experience. By the time they reached Dorking the rest of the field was out of sight.

Emma realised that she would have to act now or not at all. In a few miles the woodland would give way to suburbia, they would have to slow down, and even if she succeeded in dealing with Tamara and the chauffeur there would be public spirited citizens watching. The car was travelling at nearly eighty, which would keep the driver occupied for perhaps half a minute.

Tamara's hand was resting affectionately on Emma's knee. Emma put her hand on Tamara's, slipped her left hand up behind the elbow and then pulled sharply across her knees. This sent Tamara's body jerking forward and should have broken her right arm, but instead Tamara rolled onto the floor and pulled Emma on top of her.

The chauffeur must have stamped heavily on the brake because they rolled across the car and Emma was squashed against the front seat. She gasped, and that was nearly her last—Tamara put both hands round Emma's throat and squeezed. There was no room for manoeuvre. Emma simply lay there,

writhing and choking, vaguely hearing Tamara calling her a treacherous little bitch. . . .

Then quite suddenly the grip was relaxed and
Tamara slid to the floor beside her.

"You nearly got yourself killed," the chauffeur
said irritably. "Why did you interfere?"

Emma glanced wearily at the spanner in his hand.
"I had no intention of going to America."

"I wasn't taking you to America." The chauffeur
walked round and climbed into his driving seat. "If
she starts coming round just hit her again, and don't
bungle it this time."

"Where are we going?"

"Scotland Yard."

"Who are you?"

"The name's Romansky." He was the laconic type.
The high speed flight across suburbia continued
and they reached the Thames Embankment in another half an hour. It didn't seem worth arguing
with him when the police were at hand.

The police, of course, were delighted to see
Tamara and they took her straight into the interview room. But they weren't overwhelmed by Emma's importance, and when she insisted that they
raid the Old Barn to rescue Steed they told her to
wait, Mrs. Montalbain.

"My name is Emma Peel—"

"Is this your photograph?" they asked, pointing to
the forged passport. "So wait here. You can answer
a few questions when we're ready."

Romansky claimed to be a private citizen doing
his duty, and he told the police he wanted his name

kept out of this. "Just tell anyone who asks that we were stopped for speeding, and your brilliant man on point duty recognised Tamara Petrova," he said confidentially.

"If you'll wait here, sir, I must contact some-one. . . ."

"You needn't bring the M.I.5 into this—"

"Just relax, sir. We know our business."

Steed saw a man's body disintegrate, a leg floated away from his thigh and his head exploded, while music after the style of Webern plinked and plonked on the sound track. A dozen obscene shapes floated across the walls and assembled on the ceiling into a picture of a woman, and that floated down as if it would smother him. Then a blinding flash destroyed the recognisable shapes in vivid flames.

He knew the technique; it was meant to undermine his recognition of order, as the surrealists had wanted to, by giving people faces like cauliflowers or bodies assembled in a different way to destroy confidence in normality. Normality, after all, is what we are accustomed to, and if we become accustomed to a head expanding like a balloon until it bursts, then that is normal.

Words flashed across the screen; DUTY, DUSTY, DIRTY, DUTY, BEAUTY, DIRTY. And an advertisement for a beautiful fountain pen became a phallic symbol, grew, exploded. BEAUTY, DIRTY, DUTY. The phallic symbol exploded again, and screams buckled the sound track. Steed relaxed; it was the answer to all problems. With the more harmless (non-physical) forms of brainwashing the way to avert real damage is to succumb immediately. It was like agreeing to everybody and everything—you agree to nothing. Steed relaxed and closed his eyes, but not for long. A sudden white flash made him flinch and open them. And the effort was just as wearing on his nerves as the film show. People turned into reptiles, and lizards spoke with the words of men. In a few hours this could become disturbing.

Somebody had read their Freud; a slipper became a mouth that devoured a small man whole, a woman became a tarantula and a baby with teeth chewed a lemon. Steed never had liked the cinema very much, and Shin Peng's back row reassurances, "Just submit, Mr. Steed, don't fight it," made him shudder.

"So you're the notorious Mrs. Peel! Well well well. As dramatic as rumour has it! I suppose you wouldn't oblige me by tearing up a telephone directory—"

"I don't know who you are," Emma snapped angrily, "but I've been kept waiting at this police station for over an hour!"

"The name's Fletcher, M.I.5," he said, stretching out a limp paw. "And good moments, as they say. . . ."

"Every minute that you waste is further colossal pain for John Steed—"

"Really?" He sounded fascinated.

Emma told him about the basement in Sussex,

and Fletcher chuckled indulgently. "Old Steed played a little prank on one of my men—"

"If you don't do something immediately I'll scream!"

"Tear up a telephone directory," he urged.

Emma flopped into a chair and forced herself to relax. "All right," she sighed, "how do you come into this?"

"Me? I've been in it since S.H. kicked the frying pan. By the way, do you know the route to Rochford? There aren't any hundred foot cliffs or any high bridges, that sort of thing. . . . No, I feared not. We shall have to mock up a car crash. Let's drift along to the interview room and see whether Tamara Whosit and her chauffeur have had their elevenses."

The tall, effete and exasperating Fletcher ambled out of the room whistling 'Greensleeves'. "I'll see whether we can get old Steed out of that place, but of course we can't upset Mr. Krystal. Have to be discreet, you know." He stopped complacently before the sleeping bodies of Tamara and the chauffeur.

"Are they drugged?" Emma asked.

"L.S.D., I'm afraid. They're both well known addicts."

"Are they?"

"Oh yes, the F.B.I. have them on their records. Rick was arrested twice in 1964 and Billie was treated for an overdose last year. Never been inside, but that's the Mafia for you. Very influential chaps in the States, like the two hundred."

"Rick and Billie?" said Emma, confused.

"Yes, the Montalbains." Fletcher smiled proudly. "That's who our two friends back there are going to be for the purposes of one very fatal car crash."

On their way out Fletcher checked on the desk sergeant's record book. It showed that 'Rick' and 'Billie Montalbain' had been brought in for speeding, and that they left again at 12.30 to continue their journey. Emma helped carry them out the back way.

The kandy koloured tangerine thing was driven by a sinister character with a cold in the head. He introduced himself as Bickerton, and he spluttered feverishly when he was told that Emma was a colleague of John Steed.

Emma and Fletcher followed behind in an inconspicuous Jaguar. They spent nearly an hour trying to find somewhere suitable, and during that time Emma could only discover that the chauffeur was a Russian agent. Fletcher didn't talk very much about his work, although he talked a lot.

"I've got it!" said Emma excitedly. "The chauffeur, or Romansky, whatever his name is, wanted Tamara brought to trial in this country. Scandal, sensation and so on."

"Maybe," said Fletcher.

"That's roughly the same thing as Krystal wanted: scandal, sensation and so on, but he didn't want Tamara done as a spy."

"Done?"

"And you, I suppose, are hushing the whole thing up!"

Fletcher smiled.

A few miles from Rochford they stopped, and Bickerton gave them an expert demonstration of the game of chicken. It was a deserted country road with a sharp right turn. If you didn't turn right you would hit one of those concrete pill boxes that still litter fields a few miles from the coast, relics of the wartime fear of invasion.

Bickerton arranged 'Rick' and 'Billie' in the front seats, then he sat on 'Rick's' lap and drove the gaudy car at thirty, forty, nearly fifty miles an hour down the lane. At the last possible moment he opened the car door and rolled out onto the grass verge. He carried on rolling for sixteen feet and came to a stop in the ditch. The car shot up the grass bank, crashed through the wooden fence and then crunched into the concrete pill box. The noise was sickening and Emma looked away.

When she turned back the car was enveloped in flames, and she could still see the fire from the Western Avenue as they drove back to London. Then they went round a slight hill and it was all over. Officially it had never even happened.

Steed found that he wasn't suffering any more. His mind was slipping and snapping from one subject to another and from this kind of awareness to that level of consciousness. Things happened, like he was asked who he was and he didn't quite remember, and he was hit on the soles of his feet with a rod and he thought they had done that to him before, only *maybe* this was before.

Someone had told him he always obeyed what Curt Krystal instructed him to do. Did he? Yes, probably he did. Well, it was a good trait, showed discipline. "This is an instruction. . . ." That's a good lad. He couldn't remember who Krystal was, but the voice droned on, and a soothing female voice told him to relax and that was nice. Steed couldn't work out why he was so unhappy. But they said he had been naughty.

"Are you going to do as you're told?"

"Yes, sir."

That was when he was a boy, a few minutes ago, and it was too much of a strain. All those people to please, all those men who hit you for saying the wrong thing and women who suddenly grow cold and you don't know why. So much to learn. Why do mothers grow indifferent, and why do men hit you all the time? I'm trying, really I am, the English taught the Russians to fight and now the Russians are the best soldiers in the world. I didn't mean to wet myself. Russia is the best country in the world. No no, please, I won't do it again!

That was a strain. But now it was much earlier; familiar though. Nice. No sight, no sound, and he couldn't feel anything. Or maybe he could feel something womb-like all over him, all round, and maybe he could see blackness. There was no up or down or sideways, no weight or direction. He just was. There was no memory; where am I? here, this is all. It was nice.

No! Please don't . . . what's happening? I don't want to be born! Please. . . .

Steed was floating in a tank of water with his breathing apparatus leading into his rubber suit like an umbilical cord. Emma had kicked Curt Krystal in the groin as he came up the stairs towards her, and then she had felt her way through the folds of flesh in his neck to stop the blood to his head. He had fainted without more than a grunt. But now Emma was angry. Steed had mufflers over his eyes and ears, things like boxing gloves on his hands to kill the sense of touch, and she knew what that treatment did to the mind. She turned to face the three Chinese girls feeling very ruthless.

They were evenly matched. Emma ducked and twisted as the first one came at her; she threw her straight over the left shoulder, but the Chinese girl landed perfectly and then came at her from behind. Emma quickly allowed the second girl to give her an expert stomach throw, then she rolled to the third and brought her down with her feet before the girl had worked out who was who. It was slightly absurd, and an audience would have applauded all four of them.

Fletcher wasn't watching, however; he was staring at the tank and trying to prod Steed with his umbrella. A Chinese girl landed against his legs as he moved aside. "Careful," he murmured, "this is valuable equipment." He pulled the breathing apparatus and Steed floated gently to the top.

"Pinkerton!" he called. Pinkerton came down into the cellar. "Help me lift this fellow across the room, over to that couch."

"Have you seen the other room, sir?" asked

Pinkerton gravely. "It's like a morgue. Seven or eight people, just lying there, alive . . . in some kind of trance."

Steed struggled weakly as they lifted him out. "No! Please don't . . . what's happening?" He was shouting something idiotic about being born as he realised that two men were taking a hood off his face. He blinked nervously. "What's all this?" He could see women flying all over the room, leaping about and shouting. Then one of the men fetched him a drink of burning liquid that hit the top of his head and made everything spin again.

Next time he focused his eyes on the room the aerobatics had stopped. A girl in a white baggy trouser suit was lying in a corner, another was being held by the tall, thin man who kept sneezing, and another was in that tank of water.

"Mrs. Peel," the other man snapped, "be careful of her! Trained operatives of her standard are hard to come by. Stop pushing her under!"

Mrs. Peel? Yes, that sounded familiar. She was smiling at him. "We're all safe now," she said reassuringly. Yes, he knew her. Nice. He let her help him off the couch and they went upstairs together.

13

It was raining in Brawhill on polling day, but Steed wasn't worried about its affect on the voting. He had told Horace Wilson that his mind had been changed. "Changed? You can't just vanish during the last three days of the campaign. . . . Take my word for it, you'll come bottom of the list." Steed hoped to God he was right.

At midnight he went with Emma to the town hall. It was part of the ritual, to hear the town clerk stumble over the results and then to make politely meaningless speeches about the wisdom of the electorate. The city square was crowded with avid listeners who put politics before personal comfort.

"They're having a re-count," a party drudge hissed as they pushed their way up the steps.

"Mr. Steed," said a town hall official, "there's an American couple asking to see you. . . ."

"Where are they?"

The official pointed across the entrance hall to Rick and Billie Montalbain. "They told me a very strange story about being officially dead. They think you are the only person who can help them."

Steed adjusted his bowler, cleared an escape route with his umbrella and pulled Emma off in the opposite direction. "Tell them to write to their M.P." he called. "I'm busy at the moment."

"You can't leave them to roam the English countryside with no official existence," Emma gasped. "After all, they are alive."

"What I always say is," Steed pronounced aphoristically, "that if you're still alive you haven't much to complain about."

The other two candidates loomed out of the counting station to exchange the correct chat with Steed and to gape at Emma. She was quite sensational, in a glossy black bombe hat with a silver buckle that matched her knee length aluminium boots. The dark glasses, unnecessary at midnight, seemed restrained compared with her black and mauve Lister fun-fur coat. The Liberal candidate gasped, and extended a tentative hand.

"We don't come across many women in politics," he stammered. "They're mostly female impersonators."

"What does that make the rest of us?" asked the third candidate. His name was Grahame. "How much would you stake on your chances for the seat, Steed?"

"Nothing," Emma intruded puritanically. "The only game Steed plays is solitaire, and that he always wins."

The town crier's voice rang out above the din, praying silence for the returning officer. Ladies and gentlemen, the results are now ready. Steed followed his two opponents onto the platform with an ominous feeling of dread, and Croupier Peel's reassuring smile only made him feel worse. Perhaps he had gambled away his freedom?

"The results of the election to parliament for the constituency of Brawhill are as follows:

<pre>
        P. J. Appleby   17,975
        R. S. Grahame   10,508
        J. P. Steed   17,905
</pre>

I hereby declare that Mr. Appleby is therefore elected . . ."

The crowds cheered and the television cameras whirred, the reporters went wild in an effort to get close to the Liberal member for Brawhill. The opinion pollsters paled and the psephologists began talking of straws in the wind. Steed unscrewed the handle of his umbrella and took a swig of brandy. The occasion called for a celebration.

"You've thrown the seat away," Horace Wilson bewailed. "You've given it to the Liberals on a silver platter."

"Come come, where's your sportsmanship?" Steed snapped. "Be British. Treat those two imposters just the same, as somebody once said."

"Okay," Wilson snarled, "now it's your turn to be British about defeat. You have to make a speech conceding victory."

Steed beamed sportingly and shook hands with the Liberal. Then he said how much he had enjoyed the campaign. "I only hope for Appleby's sake that he gets to Westminster in time. They seem to be pulling down St. Pancras Station, and I've heard that described as an omen. When St. Pancras Station is gone then the Albert Memorial can't be far behind, and after that comes the Palace of Westminster. Anarchy is overtaking us by stealth, and Appleby is our man to stem the tide. . . ."

The audience, knowing that everything Steed said was a colossal joke, roared appreciatively. It made him wonder whether he really was serious. "Whenever anybody laughs at me, to paraphrase the master, I always feel that I must be right." Ha ha, bravo. "Now that this election is over I'd like to tell you that politics is bunk. As Henry Ford once said. Or to quote Goering, whenever anybody mentions compromise I reach for my revolver." Jolly good. What a wag. And the crowd applauded. "Because there has only ever been one serious book about politics; not Marx or Keynes or your damned memoirs—*The Soul of Man under Socialism* by Wilde is the only serious book ever written on the subject. Perhaps in a hundred years you will vote for a man who stands for that, and until then . . . goodbye."

As Steed left the hall with Emma he could hear Grahame trying to capitalise on the speech by claiming that *he* was the Labour candidate. . . .

In the wet side street a newspaper hoarding flapped soggily, "Mafia boss killed in Essex crash." Emma smiled; it was better than the real truth: Mafia agent and Russian spy.

"The trouble with the Mafia," said Steed as he helped her into the Bentley, "is that they are idealists. They don't stand a chance against tough professionals. But they had a good idea."

"Which idea was that?"

"To invent a Russian who had no secret information and no Russian contacts. That was pure espionage. Unfortunately the Russians decided to make the contact."

Emma turned on the car radio, but the announcer was talking about a Liberal landslide so she turned it off again. They drove in silence out of Brawhill and into the flat Midland countryside. It was black, wet and monotonous. But their time was free; Emma had lost her job and Steed had avoided the House of Commons. She began whistling cheerfully. It seemed almost pioneering to be chugging through the deserted plains of Leicestershire in the old Bentley. Then the engine spluttered, coughed a few times, and cut out.

They were stranded.